Disaster Planning

The Midlife Crisis Series

By

Rose Bak

Table of Contents

Copyright

---

1.   https://paperorpixels.com/

About This Book

Who would have thought emergency planning would be such a disaster?

The small town of Lawson is out of compliance with a state requirement to create a disaster preparedness plan. Not wanting the town to be left unprepared for a major event, the governor sends in his top expert in emergency planning, Stephanie Holly.

Steph has spent her entire career in a field that's dominated by men. She's clawed her way to the top and she's not going to let a small-town mayor like Christopher Lawson ruin her perfect track record. She's going to get him to create a disaster plan if she has to trap him under a pile of rubble to do it.

Other than his time in the military, "Mayor Mc Grumpy" Christopher has dedicated his life to the town his family founded. Lawson is a place where people help each other without fancy plans or training exercises. He doesn't need some gal from the city coming in and telling him what his town should do. And he really doesn't need the brown-haired beauty giving him ideas about love and happily ever after, not when they come from such different worlds.

But when Steph and Christopher are forced to spend a lot of time together in close proximity, they realize that they're more alike than they ever imagined.

"Disaster Planning" is an instalove enemies-to-lovers midlife romance. If you like strong women, grumpy men with soft squishy insides, snarky banter, and nosy small-town matchmakers, check out this book today.

Join My Mailing List

Join Rose Bak's mailing list at bit.ly/RoseBakNewsletter. [2] You'll get a free book and be the first to hear about all the latest releases and special sales.

Dedication

Prologue—Steph

Christmas Eve

To: Stephanie.Holly@DEM.Colorado.gov
From: Christopher.Lawson@Mayor.Lawson.gov
Subject: State Mandated Emergency Management Plan
Miss Holly,

Your continued threatening emails are well past the point of being annoying so let me say this once and for all, as clearly as possible: I don't need you or any other liberal bureaucrat from the state telling me how to run my own damn town. Do not contact me again.

Christopher Lawson, Mayor

"How's it going, big sister?"

I glanced up as my brother Nathan walked into the kitchen looking happy and adorably rumpled. Based on the sounds I'd heard through the walls of my bedroom last night, he and his girlfriend Liz had a late night. I'd had to put my earbuds in and turn up the music to drown out what sounded like a double header of energetic sex.

Not that I minded. My little brother had always been guarded and rigid – thanks to our nightmare childhood – so it was refreshing to see him finally falling in love and opening up to someone.

His new girlfriend Liz was awesome. They'd met when Nathan, who worked for the county, came to this little town to evaluate Liz's application for a liquor license for her new café. He'd gotten trapped up here during a blizzard and after some conspiring from the townspeople, he'd fallen in love with his adversary.

I'd come along to spend Christmas in Pine Bluff with the new couple. I'd been dying to meet the woman who'd captured my little brother's heart. Liz was a few years older than my brother and totally feisty. Nathan wasn't the only person who'd fallen in love with her immediately. I had a feeling I'd be calling her "sister" by next Christmas.

"I'm fine." I answered my brother's question with a sigh of frustration that belied my words. "Merry Christmas Eve."

"You too. Why do you look so grumpy?" he asked. "That's usually my default, not yours."

It's true. While Nathan had a permanent scowl on his face – at least until he'd met Liz – my default was calm and neutral. I'd learned long ago not to show any emotion, and it was a skill that had served me well throughout my life.

I shook my head.

"Oh, it's nothing. I made the mistake of checking my work email since I didn't do it yesterday. I got the rudest email from some asshole named Christopher Lawson."

"Who is he?" Nathan asked as he poured himself a cup of coffee and topped off mine.

"He's the mayor of Lawson, one of the only towns in Colorado that hasn't finished its required disaster plan yet. He told me in no uncertain terms what he thinks about people from the state telling him what he should do in his 'own damn town' as he put it."

"Jeez. He sounds like a tool."

I closed my iPad and resolved to put the grumpy mayor out of my head until the holiday was over.

"Well, he's going to get a plan done whether he likes it or not. I'm just going to need to go down there and straighten him out, I guess. No sense in letting him ruin our Christmas though."

Christopher

One month later...

I stared at the computer monitor, rubbing my temples. These damned spreadsheets always gave me a headache. I'd much rather be outside doing something active, but a mayor's work was never done, even in a tiny town like Lawson.

My family had founded this town over a hundred years ago, eager to carve out some space in the mountains where they could engage in activities they loved, like hunting, fishing, and running illegal distilleries. As the town grew during the first half of the nineteen hundreds, we'd eventually gone legit. Mostly.

Our town had just over two thousand residents now, and every one of them was a little bit crazy. But in a good way. I'd lived here my whole life, other than my four-year stint in the Army. We were ideally situated: just far enough away to have the privacy most of us craved, but close enough that we could drive down to Denver for the day if we wanted.

I'd trained as an architect, but somehow, I'd wound up as mayor after my father passed away. I couldn't say I particularly liked the job, but when you're called to public service, you go. I guess I hadn't been surprised when the citizens of Lawson had demanded I run for mayor after my father's death, what with me being the eldest Lawson son, but I wasn't thrilled about it either.

The part I hated the most was the administrative work, and I had a full day of it scheduled. I was startled out of my focus on the quarterly budget report by a knock on the door. I knew without looking up whoever was at the door wasn't a Lawson resident. No one who lived here would bother with knocking. We weren't much on ceremony up here in Lawson.

Glancing up, I saw a fuzzy figure and my entire body started buzzing. That was weird. I hoped I wasn't having a heart attack. That was what had killed my father when he was only a few years older than me.

I removed my reading glasses and the woman in the doorway came into focus. She had a look that I'd call "girl next door". She looked to be about average height, with dark brown hair pulled back into a ponytail and large blue eyes fringed by dark lashes. Her skin was white and smooth, her expression completely neutral. I couldn't peg her age, but I'd guess late thirties, maybe early forties. Definitely younger than my fifty years.

The woman was wearing plain khaki pants, heavy duty snow boots, and a dark green puffy coat open to reveal a white button-down blouse. Her clothing was utilitarian, but that didn't stop me from noticing curvy hips and breasts that looked like a nice handful.

"Are you Christopher Lawson?"

Her voice was a little deeper than I would have expected, a little sultry, and it did funny things to my stomach. There was something about her that I couldn't define. It was a feeling, almost like I'd known her forever, which was impossible, because I'd never seen her before in my life. I was quite certain I would not forget meeting her.

"Yes. Who are you?"

"I'm Stephanie Holly from the Colorado Department of Emergency Management."

My fascination with her immediately turned to irritation.

"How the hell did you get in here?" I asked, as if the city offices were Fort Knox.

A tiny line formed between her arched eyebrows, the only sign that she was irritated at my response.

"The door was open, and no one was in the lobby."

Oh yeah, my receptionist and assistant would have gone to lunch by now. Or wandered down to the coffee shop up the street to gossip with her friends for a while.

"You should have made an appointment."

She strode confidently into my office, as if she owned the place.

"I requested an appointment with you several times, a request which you ignored," she reminded me. "You left me with no choice but to come up here unannounced."

I gave her my best glare, the one that had earned me the nickname "Mayor Mc Grumpy". It had no effect on her. She stopped in front of my desk, and I had a brief flash of myself laying her down on the scarred wooden surface and making her mine.

Where had that come from?

The bureaucrat sat herself down in one of the chairs facing my desk, making herself at home.

"As you've been repeatedly notified, Mayor Lawson, your town is not in compliance with the state legislature's directive to create a comprehensive disaster plan, leaving you in jeopardy if there's a natural or manmade disaster here in your town."

"We don't need a fancy plan Ms. Holly. Here in Lawson, we take care of our own."

"Oh really?" one eyebrow arched up. "So, if there's a train derailment on those tracks that run a few miles from here and toxic chemicals are released into Lawson's air, you and your neighbors know what to do to take care of yourselves?"

I stared at her stonily as she continued.

"If there's an earthquake here in the mountains which closes all the roads, you have a plan to provide food and medical care for up to six months while the region recovers? Helicopters won't be able to get up here with all the forest surrounding you. What if an enemy nation bombs Denver, are you prepared for the nuclear fall-out? And what if an attack on the satellite grid takes down all your communications and electricity, leaving your community dark and cut off from civilization? You're ready for that too?"

I felt my jaw drop open.

"Lady, you have a dark and disturbing imagination."

"I assure you Mayor Lawson, these are real threats that can occur anywhere, including your little town. That's why an emergency plan is so essential."

I felt the first stirring of unease. Maybe I should have read all the information the state had been sending me the last two years. Those were scenarios that had never even crossed my mind. Then I remembered how much I hated all those state bureaucrats.

"Look Lady—-," I started.

"That would be Ms. Holly," she said icily.

"Look Miss Holly," I said, deliberately ignoring her use of the honorific 'Ms.' as my eyes dropped to her bare left hand. "I don't need help from you or anyone. I'm a grown man who depends solely on himself."

We were interrupted by my assistant bustling into the office. Sending a curious glance at Stephanie Holly, she walked over to my desk and placed a brown bag on the surface.

"Here you go sweetie, I brought you lunch. One peanut butter sandwich, one turkey, just like you like." She squeezed my shoulder. "I got you a cookie too."

"Thanks Mom," I mumbled.

The bureaucrat across from me broke into a smile that took my breath away. I stared at her, feeling a thunderbolt that felt a lot like love, which made no sense at all. There was no such thing as love at first sight.

The warm feelings faded as she glanced at my lunch.

"What was that about being a grown man who depends only on himself, Mayor Lawson?"

Steph

I watched in fascination as a pink flush crept up Mayor Lawson's cheeks. He was a good looking man, totally a silver fox, with dark brown hair, almost black, with patches of silver near his temples. He had brown eyes, firm lips, a slightly crooked nose, and the most appealing scruff along his square jaw despite the fact it was only noon.

He hadn't moved from his spot behind his desk, but I could tell he was a big, burly guy, with wide shoulders and a trim waist. He was wearing a plaid shirt that strained against his biceps, the sleeves rolled up to reveal ropey forearms covered in a thin layer of dark hair. The mayor was one hundred percent male.

I wasn't usually one for older guys. I'd always dated younger men to avoid any hint of daddy issues, but something about Christopher Lawson was almost magnetic. I felt the strangest urge to curl up in his lap. At least until he opened his mouth.

"Mom, this is that gal from the state, Stephanie Holly."

I frowned. "Please avoid using sexist language around me, Mayor Lawson."

He looked confused, but his mother looked delighted. She was the opposite of him, tiny and petite with white hair cut in a chic bob that skimmed her narrow shoulders. The almond-shaped brown eyes were the only resemblance I could find between mother and son.

Mrs. Lawson reached out to shake my hand.

"Miss Holly, what a pleasure to meet you. I'm Marianne Lawson, the town secretary. What brings you to Lawson?"

"I'm here to help your town complete their required emergency management plan before the governor decides to cut all your state funding."

Behind her Christopher mumbled, "We don't need help."

We both ignored him.

"Well, isn't that nice of you to offer to help us," Mrs. Lawson said cheerfully. "We sure do appreciate that. How long does something like that take?"

"It depends on the complexity of the community and the cooperation from local officials, but for a town this size, I would say it will take about a month to create the plan and get everyone trained up."

"A month?" Christopher yelped. Again, we both ignored him.

"Will you be staying in town then, dear?"

"I figured I'd come up for the day to get started, then drive back and forth between here and Denver as needed."

"Oh no, that's not a good plan, dear. Denver is at least an hour away, longer when there's a lot of snow. You'll spend half your time in the car."

"Mom..." Christopher's voice held a warning I didn't understand.

"Christopher has an apartment over his garage."

"Mom..."

"He uses it as an Airbnb, but I know it's open all this month because I manage the bookings for him. You can stay there right next to Christopher."

"Mom..."

I glanced between them, trying to figure out what the undercurrent was. Growing up in a home with a father who was prone to violent fits of temper, I'd learned at a very young age to be aware of changes in people's moods. I sensed exasperation from Christopher and some kind of ulterior motive from Marianne, but not any anger. Regardless, I wanted no part of whatever this was.

"That's very nice of you to offer Mrs. Lawson, but—,"

"Marianne," she interrupted me. "You don't need to get back to a husband or boyfriend every night, do you?"

She shot a pointed look at my bare left hand.

"Um. No, that's not it."

I was confused why Marianne seemed to be delighted by my answer.

"That's great, if no one's waiting for you in Denver then there's no problem staying here in town while you work on the planning. I think you'll love it here."

"The state won't pay for me to stay in someone's Airbnb, or anywhere that's less than a two-hour drive away from the Capitol."

"That's no problem at all, dear. You can stay there for free for as long as you need. We wouldn't dream of charging you when you're here to help us, would we, Christopher?"

"Mom..."

Marianne continued to ignore him. She pulled her phone out of her pocket and tapped for a minute before returning her attention to me.

"I just messaged Patrick. He's my youngest and the head of Fire and Rescue. He's coming right over to give you a tour of town and help you get your bearings since Christopher has a meeting with our budget director in a few minutes."

I glanced over at Christopher. His face was stony, but his eyes flashed with irritation. Hopefully, everyone else in town would be as helpful as Marianne. It would make my job here so much easier.

"While we wait for him to get here, let's go to my desk and I'll help you get scheduled with everyone you need to work on your plan. Then you can go home and pack a bag, and you and Christopher can get started working on your plan in the morning."

"Are you sure it's okay to stay in the Airbnb?" I asked, my eyes bouncing between the mayor and his mother. "I'd really hate to impose on you."

I had to admit, I wouldn't mind not driving back and forth to Denver every day for the next month. It would make for some long days.

"We'd love to have you, dear. Truly," Mrs. Lawson responded.

"Okay, that sounds good, thank you." I turned back to Christopher. "I'll be back tomorrow then, Mayor Lawson."

Then I made a big mistake. I reached over the desk to offer him my hand. Automatically he stood up to shake my hand, his giant paw completely surrounding my smaller hand. The minute our palms touched I felt a shot of heat that went right from my hand to my core. I gasped softly, meeting his dark eyes. He looked as confused as I felt. It took all of my willpower to pull away.

As I followed Marianne out of the office, I couldn't resist looking back. Christopher stood stock still, staring at his empty hand.

Christopher

I wasn't sure what had just happened, but I was sure about one thing: my mother was playing matchmaker.

I stalked out of my office to find Stephanie chatting with my brother. The fire department was just next door, so it didn't take long to get here. Patrick was leaning in, his expression flirty. Ignoring the glare I sent in his direction, he led Stephanie out of the office.

"Mom, what was that?" I grumbled as soon as they left.

"I'm helping Stephanie get her plan done, dear. We don't want to lose our funding now, do we?"

"She doesn't need to stay in my rental to do that."

Mom sent me an appraising look. "If you don't want her staying at your place, I can ask Andrew, he's got that suite in his basement."

Something that felt a lot like jealousy burned in my gut.

"She's not staying with Andrew," I said firmly.

Our middle brother was a notorious ladies' man. He could charm any straight woman alive right out of her panties, and him charming Stephanie out of hers did not sit right with me.

"A-ha! I knew it!" My mother pointed at me with a big smile. "You like her."

"I don't like her," I lied.

I could still feel my palm tingling from where she shook my hand.

"Christopher Angelo Lawson do not lie to your mother. I knew it the minute I walked into your office, she's the one for you. You felt the Lawson Lightning Bolt."

My eyes rolled back in my head so fast I almost felt dizzy. The Lawson Lightning Bolt was a legend in my family. When a Lawson met their soulmate, they supposedly felt like they'd been struck by lightning. But I was fifty years old. I damn well didn't believe in romantic notions like lightning bolts and soulmates.

My palm tingled again, calling me a liar. I shoved it in my pocket.

"I'm not falling in love with one of the governor's stooges who has only come to town to tell us what to do."

"Okay honey if you say so. Maybe Andrew or Patrick will feel it then, and I can finally get at least one of my boys settled down before I die."

"You're not going to die, Mom."

"I'm seventy-two years old honey, of course I'm going to die. Sooner rather than later, I imagine."

"You're going to outlive us all."

I fervently believed that. Despite her age, my mother had more energy than all three of her sons combined. She ran this town more than I did, truth be told.

"All I ask if that you keep an open mind, Christopher. The universe doesn't send you a soulmate every day."

***

Stephanie Holly rolled into town just before nine the next morning. Today she was wearing black wool pants and a dark blue sweater that brought out the blue of her eyes.

"Good morning, Stephanie," Mom called as the bureaucrat parked and got out of her car. "Did you bring your suitcase?"

"Yes. And please call me Steph."

"Okay, Steph. Why don't you come with us to get some coffee and then I'll get you and Christopher started on your work."

The three of us walked down the street to the coffee shop, Steph between me and my mother. Her shoulder brushed mine, and damned if I didn't feel it all the way down my spine.

The coffee shop, ironically called 'The Coffee Shop', was run by my mother's friend Marcella. The two women greeted each other like it had been years since they'd been together, instead of just yesterday.

After ordering a black coffee to match my own, Steph and I headed back to the Municipal Building with my mom, who was chattering away about Lawson the entire time. Mom got us set up in a conference room adjacent to my office.

Opening her bag, Steph slid a light blue binder towards me, the pages arranged between a neat row of clearly labeled dividers.

"We'll start here," she said, her voice all business. "Marianne gave me some information, but let's fill in the blanks."

We spent the next three hours creating a list of contact people, identifying and prioritizing essential town services to focus on in an emergency, and laying out the plan for completing a comprehensive risk assessment and response plan. Steph was focused and smart, and I was impressed. She clearly knew her stuff.

I was man enough to admit that I should have done this work long ago. It had been irresponsible and arrogant of me to assume that we didn't need a plan.

"How about some lunch?" My mother interrupted my thoughts. "I can get you two some carry out."

Steph glanced at her phone, seeming surprised at the time.

"Oh no, I'm fine, thank you."

"You need to eat, dear."

"I'll grab a yogurt later."

For some reason that didn't set right with me. I felt an overwhelming urge to take care of this woman that I refused to consider too carefully.

"We'll both have club sandwiches."

Steph's eyes flashed. "No I won't. And I'll order for myself, thank you very much."

"Then order something."

My tone was unyielding and for just a second, I could see a flash of annoyance in Steph's eyes. She turned to my mother and gave her a polite smile.

"I'll have a yogurt please. Plain Greek yogurt if they have it, otherwise any flavor is fine."

"You don't like yogurt."

Steph's head snapped back in my direction.

"Excuse me? I'm pretty sure I do."

"No one really likes yogurt," I said confidently.

Steph and my mother both frowned at me.

"Would you like some homemade granola with that, dear?" My mother asked, clearly choosing a side. "Marcella makes some for the coffee shop."

"That would be lovely, thank you."

I watched Steph pick at her yogurt and granola for a good fifteen minutes before I couldn't take it anymore.

"Are you one of those girls who doesn't like to eat in front of a man?" I demanded.

"Excuse me?"

I nodded at her half-finished yogurt.

"Mayor Lawson—-,"

"Christopher."

If my interruption registered, she didn't react.

"First of all, I'm not a girl and I don't appreciate your sexist language or personal inquiries in a business setting."

Her scolding tone made my cock press against the zipper of my pants.

"Second, I don't need to justify my lunch choices to you or anyone else. Let's just stay focused on our work."

I felt a grudging admiration for her. With the exception of my mother and brothers, no one ever stood up to me.

"Fine. I apologize. But I still don't believe that you like yogurt."

Steph

God, I needed to take my own advice and focus on my work. I'd always been laser focused. Driven. Single minded even. All throughout school, throughout my career, it had been the same. But something about Christopher Lawson was really messing with my concentration. And it pissed me off.

Trapped here in this conference room with him, every once in a while I'd catch a whiff of his outdoorsy aftershave. I wanted to bathe in that scent. Several times I'd found myself staring at him, wondering what his story was, instead of focusing on the task at hand.

Marianne brought us in a couple of bottles of water midday, looking curiously between us. She seemed awesome, but I had a sneaking suspicion she was trying to fix me up with her grumpy son.

I didn't know how I could break it to her that I wasn't the cheerful little sunshine who would marry him and brighten his world. Christopher had accused me of having dark thoughts yesterday, and he wasn't wrong. I'd made a career out of worrying about what bad things could happen.

It was a great skill in an emergency manager. That's what we did: we thought of everything that could possibly go wrong and developed a comprehensive plan to respond if it happened. Planning made me feel safe. And I didn't need to be a psychologist to figure out why.

Forcing myself to concentrate on the task at hand, I worked another hour with Christopher before heading over to the medical building. I had a meeting with the town's only doctor to start creating a medical triage plan.

I'd made arrangements to meet Christopher at his house just after five o'clock so he could give me the keys and show me around the rental his mother had offered. After that, I planned to relax. I'd be lying if I said I wasn't looking forward to spending a few hours alone. I was an introvert, and peopling was hard for me. Peopling with someone as attractive as Christopher Lawson was even harder.

Christopher lived at the far edge of a cul de sac that looked like it was carved into the forest, each of the houses backing up to a wooded area. The house itself had a stone façade and a wraparound porch that I immediately longed to sit on with a cup of tea and a good book.

"Welcome," Christopher greeted me, his tone not particularly welcoming. He looked like he'd rather be literally anywhere else right now.

He pointed at a staircase built onto the side of the garage.

"The unit's upstairs," he said. "Let me get your bags."

"I've got it," I said, slinging my duffle bag over one shoulder, my laptop bag over the other.

"That's all you've got?" he asked. "You pack light for a g—, you pack light."

"I'm only here for a few days," I reminded him. "I'll go back to Denver for the weekend."

He tugged at my duffle bag, and I resisted for a minute before letting him take it off my shoulder with a sigh. The side of his mouth twitched, and I wanted to punch him. If there was one thing that I hated, it was guys who treated me like I was fragile because I was a woman.

The second floor apartment was a light and airy studio with large windows, bright paint, and comfortable looking furniture. I liked it immediately.

"There's a bed on the other side of the half wall," he said pointing. "Bathroom and kitchen have everything you need. The Wi-Fi password is on the refrigerator. Help yourself to anything in the cabinets. Your keys are on the counter."

"Thank you."

He stood in the center of the room for a long moment, and my eyes rose to his. I felt trapped in his gaze, and suddenly the apartment seemed much smaller. The air between us felt warmer, almost charged with electricity like there was going to be a storm.

I had the strongest urge to move closer to him. I couldn't deny that as much as Christopher's personality repelled me, physically I was attracted to him. And that really pissed me off.

"Anything else I need to know?" I asked when I couldn't take the silence anymore.

"No," he bit off. I couldn't read his mood, and I hated that.

"Thanks then," I dismissed him. "I'll see you tomorrow."

With one more inscrutable look, he was gone.

After checking out the space, I grabbed my car keys and headed back to the main street area to visit the grocery store I'd seen coming into town. I grabbed a few staples and then, on impulse, a box of HoHos, my secret vice.

When I got back to Christopher's house, I roasted a chicken breast, made a salad, and opened a bottle of red wine that I'd brought from home. While I waited for my chicken to cook, I texted my brother.

Steph: *How's it going little brother?*

Nathan: *It's going OK, but I miss Liz.*

Steph: *Are you going up there this weekend?*

Nathan: *No, she has to work at the café. I'm just in the way on the weekends.*

Steph: *It sucks having opposite schedules.*

Nathan: *Yeah, but we're planning to do something in Denver for Valentine's Day in a few weeks, so at least there's that. How's your project going?*

Steph: *Pretty good. The mayor is still resistant but the other folks that I've met so far actually seem to understand the value of my work so that's good.*

Nathan: *Where are you staying?*

Steph: *I got an Airbnb in town.*

Nathan: *The state's paying for that?*

Steph: *No, the mayor's mother, who's also the town secretary, offered it to me for free, although I think she's got an ulterior motive. She keeps talking up her son. Said if I don't like him, she's got others I can meet.*

Nathan: *LOL. Why do I see a shotgun wedding in your future?*

Steph: *Bite your tongue. You know how I feel about marriage. And small towns.*

Nathan: *Well be careful then. You know what happened to me.*

The next three days passed quickly. I worked with Marianne to create the first draft of a continuity of operations plan for municipal services in between meetings with the Fire Department, the Water Bureau, and the principals for both the elementary and high schools. As I conducted my surveys, I developed a picture of how this particular town worked. I assessed what strengths the existing systems in Lawson would bring in case of different types of emergencies, and where they'd likely need outside help.

My temporary landlord, Mayor Mc Grumpy as I'd learned the locals called him, mostly seemed to be avoiding me, preferring to have his mother and city secretary take the lead. It was for the best, since every time I had any contact with him he was curt, annoying, or argumentative – sometimes all three.

"Are you going back to Denver tonight?" Marianne asked on Friday afternoon.

I glanced at my phone, noting it was already after three o'clock. Snow had been falling steadily all day, and it would be dark in less than an hour.

"No, I think I'll wait for morning when the roads will hopefully be clearer."

"That sounds like a good idea. And that means you can come to dinner tonight. I have family dinner with the boys every Friday."

I looked up, noting the mischievous gleam in Marianne's eye that I'd already come to recognize.

"Oh, no, thanks for the invitation but I don't want to impose."

Not imposing was a big thing for me. Not spending more time with Mayor Mc Grumpy than I absolutely had to was another.

"Don't be ridiculous," Marianne said with a dismissive wave of her hand. "I'm already cooking for the boys. It won't be an imposition at all."

I'd met all three of her sons, all of them over forty and each one bigger and burlier than the last. It cracked me up that she still called them 'the boys'.

"To be honest, it would be nice to have another woman there for once," Marianne added, her tone turning pleading.

"I'm really kind of tired..."

"Then you'll appreciate having someone else cook." Marianne craned her neck and yelled, "Christopher!"

The mayor strode in a few seconds later. "You bellowed, Mom?"

"Yes. I convinced Steph to join us for family dinner. You'll give her a ride so she can find my house."

"I have GPS," I protested.

"You only live a mile away," he said at the same time.

"Perfect. Christopher will pick you up at six-fifteen," she said, completely ignoring us. "We eat at six-thirty. I'll see you both in a few hours."

Christopher

"Are you ready?"

Steph was waiting at the top of the driveway when I came out of my house at six-fourteen. At least she was punctual. Being around her all week had been torture. I kept finding myself staring at her like a lovelorn teenager, while she seemed mostly unaware of my presence.

She was wearing the same clothes she'd worn earlier, neatly pressed jeans, and a long cardigan over a tightly fitted tank top. As always, her hair was pulled back into a simple ponytail, and her face was free of make-up other than a touch of what I knew was Burt's Bees tinted lip gloss on her luscious lips.

"Yep." I noticed she was carrying a box from the bakery on Main Street.

"Whatcha got there?" I asked.

"Cookies."

Refusing my offer of a hand up, she boosted herself into the cab of my truck and settled in the passenger seat. As I slid into the driver's side, the subtle citrus scent I associated with her became more pronounced in the small space. I wondered if it was her shampoo or her body wash, which was a bad idea because that led to visions of Steph in the shower.

I was pathetic. I'd spent the whole week hyper aware that she was working right next door to me. I'd spent countless hours talking myself out of going over there to visit her. We made the short drive to my mother's house in complete silence.

Say something, idiot, I told myself a few times, but anything I thought of saying sounded stupid in my head. This woman had me totally tongue tied. Despite her neutral expression, she radiated dislike for me, and that just made me like her more. It was so confusing.

When we got to my mother's house, everyone greeted her like she was a long-lost friend. My mom gave her a big hug, and both of my brothers talked and joked around with her, completely at ease with Steph despite only knowing her for a few days. Steph was friendly and polite but seemed the tiniest bit uncomfortable.

"How was your meeting with Principal Snyder?" Patrick asked her as we all worked together to set the table and bring out the food.

I'd grown up in this house, and my father had grown up here before us. Andrew and I had bought our own places years ago, but Patrick still lived here with Mom despite just having turned forty. Andrew and I loved to give him shit about it. He'd just gotten back from the military when Dad died of a sudden heart attack in the living room, and after that, I think he'd felt guilty about leaving Mom alone in the house.

I shoved him out of the way as he tried to sit next to Steph, taking the seat for myself instead. Pat's eyebrow raised but he didn't call me on it, although I knew I'd hear about it later.

"It was great," Steph said. "We're planning some fun new emergency drills for the kids."

"Yeah that sounds fun," I grumbled. "Way to terrorize the kids."

Steph sent me that little frown I'd only seen her use on me, the one where her lips pursed slightly, and a line appeared between her eyebrows. Mom sent me a disapproving glance but didn't comment.

Mom had outdone herself with a giant pot roast she'd cooked all day in the crockpot along with potatoes and carrots. She'd made one of her 'kitchen sink' salads that involved pretty much any salad appropriate item she could find and had whipped up a batch of biscuits from scratch. My brothers and I split a six-pack of beer while my mom and Steph made their way through a bottle of red wine.

I loved my family, honestly I did, but the truth was that I'd felt like a bit of an outsider ever since my father died. He and I were always very close, while my two brothers were tight with my mom. Dad and I had shared similar personalities too, both of us quiet and introverted while my brothers were more outgoing and cheerful like our mother.

"Where's your family, Steph?" Mom asked partway through dinner.

Steph stiffened next to me. "Um. I have a brother who lives in Denver."

"What about your parents? Are they still alive?"

Another pause. "My mother passed away when I was in college."

It was only because I was sitting so close to her that I saw the brief flash of emotion on her face before she schooled her expression again.

"What about y—-?"

"Did you go to school in Denver?" I asked her a direct question for the first time all night, somehow knowing instinctively that Steph didn't want to answer the question about her father that was no doubt coming next.

She shot me a look I couldn't read. "Yeah, I went to U of C Denver," she said, referring to the state university in the Capitol. "I majored in Emergency Management and Disaster Planning."

"I never even knew that was a thing," Mom said. "Were there a lot of women in that program?"

She shook her head. "No, the Emergency Management field is almost exclusively male, and it was even more so back when I was in school. The field attracts a lot of former military guys, and the long hours and unpredictability of the work make it a difficult career for women who want families. I'm one of only two state-wide directors in the country who are female."

"What attracted you about emergency management?" Patrick asked curiously.

She paused in that way she had, like she was choosing her words carefully. "I always liked planning. Was always a person looking out for...things that could go wrong."

Her little hand was clenched in a tight fist on her thigh, the only tell that something about this conversation was difficult for her. I gave into the impulse to put my hand over it, giving her a reassuring squeeze. I considered it a victory when she didn't punch me in the junk. My skin tingled everywhere it touched hers.

"Tell us more about these emergency drills you're planning for the elementary school," I suggested.

Next to me, Steph let out a long breath, and her body relaxed. I kept my hand on top of hers for a few minutes more until she finally pulled away.

"We set up this stage to simulate an earthquake..."

Steph

"Thanks for dinner Marianne, I'll see you on Monday."

Dinner ended without any more invasive questions from Marianne. I was grateful that Christopher didn't linger after dinner, telling his mother he had work to do at home. It was weird, but I had the sense that he knew I didn't want to stay long, even though I'd never mentioned it.

Also weird: the way he'd somehow picked up on my discomfort talking about my family. When he'd changed the subject, I'd been grateful. When he'd cupped my hand in his, well, that had been...nice. Comforting. Arousing. And totally confusing.

As Christopher drove us back to his house, I couldn't help but reflect on how stereotypically happy his family seemed to be. It was night and day from the home I'd grown up in. There were no drunken rages, no one walking on eggshells trying to anger anyone. Just a lot of teasing between the brothers, a nosy mother, and a strong sense of love.

I wasn't a person who'd had a lot of experience with other people's families. Even with close friends and guys I dated, I tried to avoid any situation that involved spending time with their families. It always felt like too much work to figure out the dynamics, leaving me feeling anxious. But at the Lawson home, I'd felt completely at ease.

Just like on the way over to his mother's, Christopher was completely silent on the short drive back to his house. I didn't mind the silence though, it didn't feel uncomfortable. He finally spoke as we turned up his street.

"Thanks for coming to dinner," he said, his voice a little scratchy. "My mom loves getting a little more estrogen in the house."

"So I gather. She's very disappointed that none of you are married," I said.

"Oh, we're all painfully aware of that," he said drily. "I'm sure she's scheming about how to pawn you off on one of us."

I wasn't completely sure how flattering that was, but I decided to take it at face value.

"Yeah, I picked up on that. I tried to tell her that I never want to get married, but she seems to think the problem is that I just haven't met the right man yet. The fact that I live and work in Denver doesn't seem to be a barrier for her either."

"Sorry about that."

"It's totally fine. I'm only in town for a short time anyway. Honestly, dealing with your matchmaking mother is a piece of cake compared to the shit I usually deal with in this job."

As one of the only women in authority in an alpha male dominated field, I dealt with a lot of sexism and territorialism. Sometimes it was exhausting.

We pulled into the driveway.

"What time are you leaving in the morning?" Christopher asked.

"Whenever I get up, I guess."

"Is everything okay in your car? You've had it checked recently?"

I couldn't decide whether I was annoyed or touched by his apparent concern.

"Yeah, I'm good. I need to keep my vehicle in good condition and ready to go at any time with my job."

I hopped out of the truck and the next thing I knew I was flat on my back staring up at the starry sky, with my lower legs trapped underneath the truck. I'd only narrowly avoided slamming my head on the concrete.

"Steph? What the hell?"

Christopher ran over to my side. "Are you okay?"

I shot him an embarrassed grin. "Yeah, I just hit a patch of black ice before I realized what was happening."

"Let me pull you out."

He squatted down and grabbed me underneath the arms, gently sliding me backwards until my body was clear of the truck, then lifted me to my feet, twisting me around at the same time. I ended up standing face to face with him, our bodies only a few inches away from one another. His hands slid from underneath my arms to my hips, just beneath the hem of my puffy coat. They felt like a brand, even through the thick fabric of my pants.

"Are you sure you're not hurt?"

He sounded worried, and I tried not to read too much into that.

"No, I'm fine."

My voice sounded breathless, probably because my heart was pounding like a freight train, and not from the fall. Being this close to Christopher was messing with my head. And other parts of my body.

We stood there for what felt like a lifetime, just looking at each other. It felt incredibly intimate somehow. Finally, Christopher cleared his throat, breaking the spell.

"I guess we should get inside."

I stepped back reluctantly. "Yeah. Thanks for the ride, and for helping me up."

"No problem."

I walked around him, but I felt his eyes on me the entire way up the stairs. When I turned back, he was watching me, an intense expression on his handsome face.

After a restless night, I woke up early, eager to get back to Denver and get some breathing room. Being in Lawson was messing with my mind, making me lose the focus I'd worked so hard to cultivate. When I got down to my car, Christopher was squatting by the rear passenger side, a tire gauge in his hand.

"What are you doing?" I asked sharply.

He jumped at the sound of my voice, looking almost sheepish.

"Just making sure your tires have enough air. The pressure can change rapidly when the temperatures go up and down."

"Yeah, I know. I have an air compressor in the trunk just in case."

"How about you pop the hood and I'll check your fluids." His words sounded like he was making a suggestion, but his tone was more like an order.

"I checked the fluids before I left Monday," I told him. "Checked the belts and hoses too. I'm not some totally helpless woman you know."

"Just trying to be helpful," he said mildly.

I would never in a million years admit it, but it felt nice to have someone want to take care of me. I was usually that person for everyone else in my life, including my brother. Always had been.

Christopher walked over to me and to my shock, pulled me into a quick hug.

"Well, have a safe trip then. We'll see you Monday."

He strode away quickly, leaving me staring after him. Did Christopher "Mayor Mc Grumpy" Lawson really just hug me? What did that even mean? I pondered that question the entire ride back to Denver.

Christopher

"What's up with you and the hottie?"

I gave my brother a glare that would have wilted a lesser man.

"She has a name."

I hurtled the ball towards the basket, then cursed under my breath as I missed the shot. Somehow even when she wasn't here, Steph was messing with my life.

"Oh, I know. Steph's a cool chick but Mom said you called dibs."

"Called dibs?" I stopped with the basketball under my arm, staring at my brother. "What are we? Seventeen? You don't call dibs on a woman, dipshit."

He smirked. "You like her."

"I don't like anyone. Including you."

He batted the ball out from beneath my arm and started dribbling.

"You seemed different last night at dinner. Not as grumpy as usual. You asked questions, and even spoke more than one sentence at a time. I was impressed."

I chased him up the court, cursing under my breath as he easily sank the ball into the basket.

"I wasn't different," I denied.

I was a liar. I was totally different, because for the first time in my life, I was in love. As my mother suspected, I'd felt the Lawson Lightning Bolt. And just my luck, it was with a woman who didn't seem to particularly like me and lived an hour away from me to boot.

I was totally fucked.

The next week passed quickly. I'd had my mom clear almost everything from my schedule so I could work with her and Steph on our emergency plan. When I'd been in the military I'd learned about exposure therapy. They'd take a guy who was afraid of spiders or snakes and make him come into contact with them over and over again until they lost their power. That's what I wanted to do with Steph.

Besides, we actually had a lot of work to do, thanks to my previous procrastination.

Unfortunately, by the time Friday came around I had to admit that my exposure therapy plan wasn't working. Being around Steph every day just made me more obsessed with her.

"Jesus, you're eating yogurt again?" I griped as I came into the conference room that afternoon.

Why couldn't this woman eat a proper meal for lunch? Steph looked up from her laptop, licking her spoon. My gaze fixed on her little pink tongue as it swiped the last of the yogurt off the white plastic. Suddenly my pants felt a little tight.

"You know my mom will get you anything you want for lunch," I reminded her.

"I don't like to be a bother."

Not being a bother was a very big thing to Steph. She'd used that as an excuse for multiple things over the last two weeks.

"My mom said I should bring you to family dinner tonight," I said. "She said you can drive to Denver tomorrow morning."

My brothers and I had dinner at my Mom's house every Friday night. My mother insisted on it. Not that I would admit this to my mother, but I appreciated our weekly family time, and I was looking forward to bringing Steph again.

When she opened her mouth to object, I raised my palm.

"I'm just the messenger. If you want to break her heart, you'll have to tell her yourself."

Steph rolled her eyes. "Fine. Can we review the section of the plan that deals with the impact of sunspots and attacks on satellites interrupting communications?"

"I'd like nothing better," I teased.

I'd never thought about how many things could go wrong in a town like Lawson until Steph had started working with us on the disaster plan. It seemed a little excessive to plan for so many different types of emergencies that would never happen, but I had to admit that Steph was probably right when she said we'd be glad we had a plan in place if things ever went sideways.

The reality was that the plan was basically the same for everything. The response and focus would be different for an earthquake than a nuclear attack of course, but we'd still implement our newly deputized Incident Command Team and attend to the most critical needs for the event.

I knew from my military days that going into a situation knowing who was responsible for what, and who their back-ups were, would save time and reduce confusion if something serious happened.

"Next week I'll do a training for you and the other leaders on the FEMA forms and mutual aid requests," Steph said as we wrapped up her questions on the sunspots plan.

"Mutual aid requests?"

"It's the process for when you ask other jurisdictions for help."

"We don't ask anyone for help," I said firmly. "It's not how we do things in Lawson."

"You might need to ask for help sometime."

"We won't. In this town, we look out for our own."

Steph sighed deeply. Standing up, she began pacing back and forth.

"Let's say there's an earthquake and all of your downtown is impacted. Do you have excavators? Enough emergency personnel to search the rubble for survivors before they die of crush wounds and dehydration?"

"I'm sure everyone else would come out to help." Even I could hear the stubbornness in my voice.

"Great, so you want Jim from the grocery store making a decision about the structural integrity of a pile of rubble and assessing if moving something will crush someone?"

"Well, no."

"And if it was your mother trapped under the rubble, would you prefer she wait for days hoping someone realizes where she is, or would you like to have trained search dogs to help locate her before she dies of her injuries?"

"Search dogs would be nice," I conceded.

"You know how you do that? You officially declare an emergency. Then you transmit a mutual aid request to the county."

When I started to talk, she held up her hand to stop me. Her voice had lost its usual detachment, allowing some emotion to bleed through. The emotion was exasperation, but I'd take it.

"Then if the county doesn't have what you need, they do a mutual aid request to the state, and if the governor's office doesn't have what you need, they put in a request to the feds. And then you get excavators and water and search dogs. You get assistance from trained first responders. And you get qualified to apply for FEMA disaster funds to help you rebuild and to help the survivors with things I can guarantee you that their insurance won't cover."

She stalked over to me and pointed her finger in the direction of my chest.

"Don't you understand Christopher? Your stubborn refusal to learn the system could mean life or death for the people in this community. I'm not here to be a pain in your ass, I'm here to help you!"

On impulse, I grabbed the hand pointed in my direction. Steph immediately froze.

"I think both things are true," I whispered.

"What?"

"You're here to help, and you're also a pain in my ass, but maybe not in the way you mean."

My eyes snagged hers, and I took a step closer, until less than an inch separated our bodies. The air between us crackled. Her hand trembled in mine.

"What are you doing?" For the first time since I'd met her, Steph sounded unsure.

"Something that's probably a very bad idea."

Steph

Christopher leaned towards me, eyes dark with intent. I only had a split second to process what was happening before his lips crashed down on mine. He dropped his hold on my hand, sliding up to grip my shoulders. His lips were firm and demanding, and damned if I didn't open for him when he nipped my lower lip.

His tongue swept in against mine, and never one to be passive, I met him and dueled for control. Our kiss was passionate and wild, and my entire body was vibrating with arousal.

I'd known. Somehow, I'd just known that if we ever touched it would be like this. It was like lifting the patch on a dam and letting the water crash through. Like turning on the electricity on a downed power line and watching it snap and arc with power. The attraction that had been simmering between us burst to the surface, making me feel totally out of control.

I spent my life planning for disaster, but I'd never planned for feeling like this.

Without breaking the kiss, Christopher walked me backwards until my hips met the edge of his desk, pinning me between the desk and his large body. Somehow my arms had gone around his waist, pulling him closer, and I felt something long and hard press against the soft swell of my lower belly. My hips rolled against his in response, seeking friction.

"Are you two just about—-."

Marianne's question ended abruptly as she entered the room.

"Oops. Never mind. Carry on."

I lifted my hands and shoved my palms against Christopher's broad chest with enough force that he stumbled back a few steps. Sliding out from between him and the desk, I rushed past Marianne.

"Steph, wait."

I grabbed my laptop from the conference table in the corner, shoving it in my bag while I was walking, and snagged my jacket on the way out the door. I didn't stop until I reached my car on the street. Breathing a sigh of relief that Christopher wasn't following me, I slammed my car in gear and turned towards Denver. I'd been planning to head home in the morning, but now I couldn't wait to get the hell out of Lawson.

As I drove home, I alternated between replaying the kiss and berating myself. Sure, Christopher had initiated the kiss, but I wasn't an unwilling participant. And God help me, what a kiss it had been. I was fairly sure I'd be remembering that kiss when I was ninety years old, even if I never saw him again. It had been rough and passionate, like he couldn't help himself. Like neither of us could. Like we'd had two weeks of fighting as foreplay leading up to the moment his lips touched mine.

Nothing like this had ever happened to me before. I'd had men make passes at me at work, and they'd each been rebuffed with strong words, and in at least two cases, a sharp knee to the groin. But of all the things I longed to do with Christopher's groin area, causing pain had been last on the list.

I couldn't decide if I was more upset that I'd behaved like that at work, or that I'd lost my control. I was always in control, over my body, my emotions, my words. Christopher seemed to be able to make me forget all of that, and I hated him for it. Being out of control was dangerous, I knew that more than anyone.

My father had control issues. He'd always been prone to anger, especially when he was drinking. Then the factory near our small town had closed, plunging the entire community into unemployment and abject poverty. The drinking had gotten worse, and so had his temper.

Nathan and I had escaped to Denver as soon as we were old enough to go to college, but our mother refused to leave. We'd begged her to divorce him, but she always made excuses for him. Right up until our father had killed her in a drunken rage. The last time I'd seen him was at his sentencing hearing. I didn't plan to see him again until they lowered him into the ground.

My brother and I had grown up to be successful despite our upbringing. We both had good jobs, were respected in our fields. We both owned our own homes. And until recently, we'd both eschewed love and long-term relationships. Then Nathan met Liz in November, and things had changed for him.

I was happy for him, but that kind of life was not for me. I wasn't going to live happily ever after in Lawson. I wasn't going to have a quickie on Mayor Mc Grumpy's desk either. I had a job to do, and I needed to suck it up, be professional, and finish this damned emergency plan so my life could go back to normal.

A weekend in Denver, back on familiar ground, was just what I needed to get my equilibrium back.

When I reached the outskirts of Denver, I voice texted my best friend, Katy. We'd been the only two women in our emergency management program in college and had immediately bonded over our experiences in a male-dominated world.

With Katy working in the county's emergency management department and me at the state, we worked together frequently in addition to being close friends. We'd spent an obscene amount of time together working in shelters for wildfire survivors and planning emergency exercises. We got each other, accepted each other exactly as we were, and could go weeks without talking and neither of us would be hurt. It was the perfect friendship.

Steph: *Hey, I know it's short notice, but have you eaten dinner yet?*

Katy: *No, I'm just walking out of pilates. Want to meet at our usual place?*

Steph: *I'll be there in about twenty minutes.*

I took the exit towards my house, pulling into the garage. Grabbing my purse, I headed out on foot, quickly covering the four blocks to

Jeannie's, my neighborhood watering hole. Katy was already in a booth in the corner when I got there, sipping what looked like a lemon drop.

I stopped at the bar for a shot of bourbon and slid into a seat across from her. Katy took one look at my face and set her drink down.

"What's wrong?"

She'd known me long enough to see past the expressionless face I presented to the world.

"I kissed someone."

She relaxed. "Is that all? I thought something bad had happened."

Katy cocked her head. "Was he too sloppy? Bad tongue control? Halitosis?"

I downed my shot of bourbon.

"The kiss was...great. Honestly, it was the best kiss of my life. The problem is that I kissed the grumpy, stubborn, and cluelessly sexist mayor of Lawson, the only town in the state that still hasn't completed its Emergency Management plan. In his office. While we were working."

Her eyes widened. "You kissed Mayor Mc Grumpy?"

"I did."

She waved her arm at the waitress approaching our table. "We're going to need a pitcher of margaritas and a huge basket of fries."

Christopher

When I got back to my house, Steph's car wasn't there, confirming my suspicion that she'd headed back to Denver already. No doubt she was as freaked out about that kiss as I was.

I paced around the house for an hour before heading over to my mother's house for family dinner. Both of my brothers were already there.

"Who pissed in your cheerios?" Andrew asked. "You look even grumpier than usual."

When I didn't answer, he added, "Does this have something to do with why your girlfriend isn't here?"

"She isn't my girlfriend," I growled.

"Not yet..."

Mom sounded giddy, her eyes bright with excitement.

"You might as well tell them," I snapped. "I know you're dying to."

"I caught Steph and Christopher kissing today," Mom told Andrew and Patrick with a huge smile on her face. "It looked very...intense."

"Then where is she?" Andrew asked.

"I think she went home to Denver. She ran out after Mom interrupted us," I said, trying and failing to not sound as miserable as I felt.

Patrick patted my shoulder.

"Are you a bad kisser?" he asked with fake sympathy. "Is that why she ran off?"

I smacked his hand away, but before I could respond, Mom did.

"Don't tease your brother, Patrick. Someday you'll be hit by the Lawson Lightning too, and it won't be so funny. Nothing good comes easily."

"Can we talk about something else?" I asked. "Anything else?"

"It'll all work out, Christopher, I'm sure of it," Mom said, reaching up to pat my cheek. "Now let's eat."

I spent the entire weekend in a funk. I texted Steph twice, but of course she didn't respond. Not that I expected her to. Meanwhile, I couldn't stop thinking about the kiss all weekend. Or thinking about whether Steph was thinking about it too.

I'd been kicked in the hip by a horse once. He'd just missed the family jewels, and I spent days alternating between re-enacting what happened in my head and thanking every God in the sky that I'd dodged a bullet. Or a horse, in this case.

It was the same with Steph. I replayed the kiss over and over again, alternating between disappointment and gratitude that my mother had walked in before I'd boosted Steph onto the desk and fucked her until we were both sated and boneless.

That would have created even more complications than the kiss did. I didn't need complications, but I had a feeling I was going to get them anyway.

By the time Monday morning rolled around, I was in a foul mood. I stomped into the office, everyone giving me a wide berth. Except my mother of course.

"Where's Steph?" I growled. "It's after nine."

"She messaged me that she'll be late today."

I stopped, immediately concerned. "Is she okay? Did her car break down or something?"

"I don't know what the delay is, dear, but I suggest you use it to get yourself under control. You look like you're about to burn the world down."

By the time Steph got to the office just after eleven I was a wreck. As soon as I heard her voice in the lobby I raced out, coming to a stop when I saw another woman with her.

I looked Steph over hungrily, taking in her basic black pants, short boots, and the jade green long-sleeved shirt that belted at the waist, visible under the puffy coat she wore. She didn't look injured.

Steph's spine stiffened when she saw me, the only outward sign that she was flustered by my perusal. I wondered what it would take to make her lose that ironclad control. Maybe my head between her legs.

"Who's this?" I growled.

"Good morning to you too," Steph rebuked in that neutral tone of hers. "Mayor Christopher Lawson, I'd like to introduce you to Katy Robertson, the director of emergency management for the city and county of Denver. Katy, this is Mayor Lawson."

My eyes remained fixed on Steph while I shook the other woman's hand.

"What brings you to Lawson, Miss Robertson?" I asked, remembering my manners.

"I asked Katy to help us with this week's tabletop exercises," Steph answered for her.

"Tabletop exercises?" I frowned, trying to remember what I'd learned about those.

"Yes dear," my mother interjected. "Remember? We're going to simulate various disasters to practice activating our Incident Command Team."

Steph smiled proudly at my mother, and I wished I could get her to smile like that for me. Just once.

"Exactly right, Marianne. Thank you."

"It's very nice of you to come help us, Miss Robertson."

Steph's eyebrows raised in surprise at my friendly tone.

"Please, call me Katy," the other woman said, giving me a speculative look that made me wonder if Katy was more than a colleague to Steph.

"Steph, may I speak to you for a moment? Privately?"

"I'm a little busy right now," she demurred.

Ignoring her protest, I grabbed her elbow, gently steering her towards my inner sanctum while studiously ignoring the way I could feel the connection between us even through her jacket and shirt. Once we were in my office, I retreated behind the safety of my desk, leaving Steph to drop into one of my visitor chairs. When I didn't speak, she raised one eyebrow at me in question.

"I just wanted to apologize," I said, my voice sounding like I'd swallowed glass. "My behavior on Friday wasn't appropriate."

She studied me for a moment, then released a small sigh.

"I kissed you back Christopher. We were both at fault. Let's just forget it ever happened and move forward with our work."

"Can you?" I leaned forward, placing my elbows on my desk.

"Can I what?"

"Forget it ever happened?"

I studied her carefully, noting the slight flush that started at her neck and worked its way up her cheeks, the only hint that this conversation was impacting her the way it was me.

"Of course," she said stiffly, her gaze studying her hands in her lap like they held the secret to the mysteries of the universe.

"Because I don't think I can forget that kiss."

Her head snapped up. "What?"

I took a deep breath. I hadn't had a lot of practice talking about my feelings, but I needed to say this.

"I'm fifty years old, Steph, much too old to play games. Kissing you, well, it told me something very important."

"What?"

"I'm falling in love with you."

Steph

I jumped out of my chair as if it was suddenly electrified.

"What?"

"I'm pretty sure you heard me," he said mildly. "And I'm as happy about it as you are."

"Let me get this straight. You're telling me that you're falling in love with me and insulting me in the space of ten seconds? Do I have that right?"

He nodded, and I resisted the urge to punch him in the throat.

My heart was thumping so hard it was making me sweat. Oh wait, I was still wearing my puffy coat. I ripped it off, tossing it in the direction of my chair while I paced back and forth.

I was equally thrilled and terrified by his declaration. Thrilled because despite his grumpy attitude and less than enlightened beliefs, I had a full-blown crush on him. And some small primitive part of me longed to feel loved by someone besides my brother. But I was also terrified because people like me didn't get to fall in love. I'd seen the damage love caused, and there was no way I was going there.

I needed to protect myself.

Finally I stopped, pointing at him before I remembered what happened the last time I pointed at him. I dropped my hand to my side and clenched my fists.

"You're not falling in love with me," I said firmly. "We don't even know each other. We don't even like each other."

"The Lawson Lightning Bolt doesn't care about all that."

"What? Lightning Bolt? Did you hit your head this morning?"

"Ask my mom. She'll tell you."

I heard a knock on the door, then Marianne stuck her head in.

"Sorry to interrupt, but we need to get ready for the tabletop exercise. Everyone will be waiting for us."

"Mom, tell Steph about the Lawson Lightning Bolt."

Marianne stepped in, closing the door, and leaning against it with a happy smile.

"When a Lawson male meets their soulmate, the first time their skin touches in some way, they feel like they've just been hit by lightning. It's how they know the person is the one meant for them. It's instant love, the forever kind. No Lawson has ever gotten divorced after being hit with the Lightning Bolt."

"No offense Marianne, but that's ridiculous."

Her smile grew. "Is it? I was here when you two shook hands for the first time, and I saw it in action. It was just like when I met my husband."

I looked between mother and son, feeling a well of panic rise in my throat before Marianne apparently took pity on me.

"Come on dear, you two can figure this out later. I'll walk with you and Katy to the community center for the exercise. Christopher will meet us over there."

Katy, Marianne, and I headed out into the cold to walk the two blocks to the community center. I ignored Katy's curious looks and tried to focus on the exercise we were about to lead.

"Are you staying overnight Katy?" Marianne asked.

The tabletop exercise would run today and all day tomorrow. My friend and colleague had agreed to help me on both days.

"Yeah, I thought I'd crash on Steph's couch, so I don't have to drive back and forth."

"Oh no, that won't do." Marianne sounded horrified. "That couch is not very comfortable."

"Believe me, Steph and I have slept on concrete floors, in tents, and in the back of pick-up trucks when we've been deployed to a disaster site. Having someplace warm and dry with furniture and an indoor bathroom is a definite step up from our usual sleeping arrangements."

"My son Andrew has an extra bedroom," Marianne said. "It's kind of like a suite, it even has its own bathroom. It's very private. You should stay with him."

"You have extra bedrooms too, don't you Marianne?" I challenged, immediately seeing her obvious matchmaking plan for my friend.

"Well, yes dear, but Patrick sleepwalks in his boxers," she said. Her eyes darted to the side, telling me that she was lying. "Katy will be much more comfortable at Andrew's. He's got a beautiful house. Did you know he's a lawyer?"

The smile Katy sent me behind Marianne's back told me she was onto the older woman's matchmaking. But I'd known her a long time and knew she would be up for a little one-time fun if she found Andrew attractive and he was agreeable. Katy was much more comfortable around strangers than I was.

"How about you let me meet this Andrew before you pair us up?" Katy suggested, calling her out in that gentle way she had.

"Don't worry, you're going to love him," Marianne promised.

The three of us worked together to set up the room for the exercise. Christopher came in about five minutes before we started, his brother Patrick in tow. They checked out the labeled tables and moved to sit with their assigned groups.

The first part of the exercise went off without a hitch, and after a short afternoon break, we gathered together to do an "after action" report and review our progress.

"Everyone works very well together," I complimented the group. "You don't seem to have the turf battles we sometimes see in these exercises. Katy and I will look forward to doing the longer exercise with you tomorrow. Please dress warm and comfortably, as we will be sending you outside to work for part of the day. Thank you all."

The group filed out, leaving me and Katy with Christopher, Patrick, and Marianne.

"I have a great idea! We should all go out for pizza tonight," Marianne suggested as if she'd just thought of it. "I reserved a table already since there'll be six of us eating."

"A table for six?" Katy asked, looking around at the five of us. I could tell from her tone she knew exactly who the other person would be.

"I'll invite Andrew. It would be good for you to meet him before you stay at his house. Besides, he works so hard at his law firm, the poor dear needs to eat."

Katy's lips twitched.

"Ah, okay then. Well Steph and I have some work to do now, what time should we meet you there?"

Christopher

I stayed at the office until it was time to meet the rest of them for pizza, half hoping that Steph would come back to the office so we could talk. Or kiss some more. I could go either way. Of course she didn't show up.

When I wasn't focusing on the tabletop exercise today, I'd vacillated between chiding myself for sharing my feelings and being happy it was finally out there. My words hadn't been completely truthful. I wasn't *falling* in love with Steph, I was firmly in love with her. Kissing her the other day had only sealed the deal for me.

Clearly, she didn't feel the same. But could she? If I could just spend some time with her and get to know her better, I hoped the path forward would become more clear.

When I got to the pizza place on Main Street, Mom was in full matchmaker mode.

"Let's sit boy-girl-boy," she said as we arrived. "Christopher, you sit here by Steph, then Patrick can sit between Steph and Katy, and we'll save this seat next to Katy for Andrew."

I guessed if Mom didn't foist Katy off on Andrew, she'd have Patrick waiting in reserve. Not that she needed to worry. The minute Andrew set eyes on Katy, he looked like he'd been smacked up the side of the head with a two-by-four.

I wasn't sure how all three of us brothers had gotten past forty without so much as an engagement, and now two of us were down for the count in less than a month. It made me wonder if another stranger was going to wander into town and sweep Patrick into this madness.

"You know," Mom announced, looking around expectantly. "Next Tuesday is Valentine's Day. Katy dear, you should come back for the Valentine's Day festival, it's so much fun."

Katy and Steph exchanged glances.

"I don't know. I'll have to check my schedule, Marianne."

After we inhaled an enormous amount of pizza, Mom turned to Steph.

"Steph dear, can you give Christopher a ride home?"

"Where's your truck?" Steph asked me, looking suspicious.

Before I could answer, Mom interrupted. "Patrick needs to borrow it."

"I do?" My brother looked confused, then he jumped, as if someone had kicked him under the table. "Oh. Yeah. I need a truck for a...thing tomorrow."

We all knew better than to argue with my mother when she got an idea in her head, so as we said goodbye, Katy headed out with Andrew, and I headed out with Steph. I slid into the passenger side of her SUV, and we drove the short distance to my house. Unable to think of something to say, I sat in silence like a doofus until Steph pulled into the driveway and got out of the car, heading towards the garage.

"Steph."

She stopped in her tracks but didn't respond. I stalked over to her, grabbing her hand and turning her around to face me. Lifting my other hand, I cupped her left cheek in my glove. She closed her eyes for the briefest moment, leaning against my fabric-covered palm.

"About what I said earlier, well, I'd like to get to know you better," I finally said. "And I'd like to have you get to know me better too. The real me, not the mayor. Let's spend some time together and see what happens."

Her eyes clouded over briefly before she did that thing she did to make her face totally neutral.

"I don't think that's a good idea Christopher. I'm going to be here another week, two tops, and then we won't see each other again."

"Unless we do."

"Christopher—."

"Tell me you didn't feel it," I said, stepping closer. "Tell me you didn't feel the Lawson Lightning Bolt. Tell me that you felt nothing when we kissed, that you haven't thought about it ever since it happened."

"Christopher—."

The mask cracked, and I saw a flash of real emotion on her face. Someday I'd understand why she was so guarded, but for right now, I wanted to take that crack in her façade and shove my way inside. I wanted to see what was behind the mask. I wanted to see the woman I loved – all of her.

Dropping her wrist, I lifted my hand to her other cheek, cupping her face between my palms, and slowly lowered my head. Last time I'd swooped in, this time when I kissed her, I wanted it to be her choice as much as mine. I needed it to be. When she didn't move, I pressed my lips against hers. They felt cold from being outside. Slanting my head, I kissed her until she sighed, letting me in, then I slid my tongue inside, gently moving against hers.

She closed the distance between us, her hands coming to my shoulders, and that was all it took for the kiss to turn hot. She kissed me with what felt like pent up frustration, her tongue tangling with mine eagerly, fighting for control.

I walked her backwards until she connected with the side of the garage, then gripped her muscular thighs, boosting her up. Her legs wrapped around my waist as if we'd been doing this for years, lining her pelvis up against the bulge in my pants.

We kissed until we were both breathless, then I nipped along her jaw while she slid her fingers through the strands of my hair. She tugged slightly, directing me back, and then we kissed again. I was hard as a rock now, grinding my cock against her core, feeling frustrated by the layers of clothing between us as we dry humped like teenagers.

"Please," she gasped when we finally pulled apart again. Her eyes were glassy.

"What do you need, baby? I'll give you anything."

"I want you. Take me inside."

Steph

Christopher looked at me like I'd just told him he'd bought the winning lottery ticket.

"Are you sure?" he asked. I'd never liked him more.

"Yes. But I can only promise tonight," I added.

"None of us is promised tomorrow," he said as he walked up the path to his house with me clinging to him like a baby monkey.

The girl in me thrilled at the easy way he handled me. I wasn't a small person, but he carried me easily, his touch gentle.

"But I'm going to try my damnedest to get it," he vowed.

Maybe it wasn't fair of me to ask for this when he'd shared his feelings with me. And the truth was, I was already feeling things for him that I'd never felt before. I'd promised myself I would stay away from him, but nothing short of a natural disaster was going to pull me away right now.

I spent my life doing things for others. Tonight, just for once, I wanted to do something for myself.

When we got to his front door, Christopher gently lowered me to my feet, finding his key and pulling me in behind him. I had a brief impression of a comfortable house with dark wood, white walls, and overstuffed furniture as we headed upstairs to what I presumed was the bedroom.

He tapped a lamp in the corner, bathing the room in soft light. I unzipped my puffy coat and pulled off my gloves, tossing them onto a nearby chair, then toed off my ankle-height boots. Christopher followed suit, then pulled his V-necked sweater over his head, leaving him in a fitted tee shirt and jeans.

When I reached for the hem of my sweater, he stopped me.

"Let me. Please."

He tugged my sweater over my head, the movement dislodging my ponytail. My hair fell past my shoulders, and Christopher ran his fingers through it, loosening the waves that I generally kept pulled back tightly.

"Beautiful," he breathed.

I went for his belt and his attention swung from my hair to the light thermal shirt I wore underneath my sweater. In seconds I stood in front of him wearing only my bra and panties, along with a pair of wool socks.

"You're wearing too many clothes," I said huskily, prompting him to remove his tee shirt and jeans.

His boxers soon followed, and his thick cock popped up towards his stomach, dripping with pre-cum. I licked my lips, my eyes widening slightly.

"Oh no," he said. "The first time I come with you, it'll be in your pussy."

I shivered at his words.

"Oh. Wait. Do you have a condom?"

I had an IUD, but I didn't want to take any chances.

"Sure do."

I felt a rush of relief. "Good."

I reached behind myself to unclasp my boring beige bra, while Christopher dropped to his knees to slide my cotton panties down my legs. I'd chosen my underwear for function, not looks, but if my mismatched undergarments bothered him, Christopher didn't let on.

Still on his knees, he leaned forward to give my pussy one long lick. I gasped, then gripped his hair as he licked me again. His tongue was wet and rough, and it was driving me wild as he explored between my lower lips. When my knees wobbled, he pulled back.

"Let's get more comfortable," he said, drawing me to his enormous bed that took up most of the room. It had to be one of those California Kings, because it looked like ten feet wide.

"Do you usually have a lot of company here?" I asked drily.

He looked confused. "If you're asking me if I've had other women here, every once in a while."

I shook my head. "This bed is big enough for like ten people," I explained. "I thought maybe you were having a reverse harem situation going on here."

"I have no idea what that means," he said. "But I like to have my space when I sleep."

"Noted."

He pushed me on my back, then shoved his way between my legs, lifting them to rest on his broad shoulders. The man was built like a lumberjack, big and bulky and muscled, other than a slight softening around his middle.

"I thought you wanted to come inside me," I said, my voice rising as he licked up my slit. God that felt good.

"My mother taught me ladies first."

I started laughing. "Do you really want to talk about your mother when your face is in my vajayjay, buddy?"

He looked up from between my thighs, his face already glistening with my juices.

"No ma'am. I sure don't."

He turned his attention back to the task at hand, gripping my thighs as he ate me out with more enthusiasm than I'd ever seen with past lovers. You could tell the guys who went down on you out of duty versus those who actually liked it. Christopher seemed to love it. And God bless him, because I loved what he was doing, so much so that it only took a few minutes of stroking me with his tongue and a nice little pinch of my clit before I was gasping his name as I came all over his face.

Christopher

I felt a primal sense of accomplishment as Steph completely lost control, thrashing beneath me, and coming with a long shudder. She wasn't vocal, but there was no doubt that she was satisfied by the time I was done.

Crawling up her body, I notched my aching cock alongside the outer edges of her pussy and did a reverse push-up over her body, lowering myself to give her a long kiss. Every touch of our lips on each other was more explosive than the last. I hadn't struggled this much to avoid coming prematurely since I was in my early twenties.

Steph was tall and curvy but lean, with more muscle tone than I'd expected. She clearly worked out with weights because I knew her day-to-day job wasn't normally physically taxing. I imagined that she needed to stay in shape for when she got called out to disaster sites though.

Suddenly Steph bent her knees and pushed. "Roll over."

I obliged, flopping onto my back. She grabbed the condom I'd found earlier and rolled it on me carefully, then moved to straddle my hips.

"I like to be on top," she said.

If it made her feel more comfortable, I was fine yielding control. I'd been studying her for two weeks now and it was clear that she was a bit of a control freak. What I didn't know was why. She'd been resistant to any prying by me or anyone else in town. And there was no one nosier than a Lawson resident. But Steph was almost as much of a mystery now as she was when she'd gotten here.

Bracing her hands on my chest, Steph began sliding her pussy back and forth over my latex-covered cock, teasing herself. Teasing me. Her full breasts bounced up and down with every movement, transfixing me.

"Baby, I don't know how long I'm going to last if you keep doing that," I warned.

"I detest diminutives," she said, but it felt like an automatic protest, no real heat behind it.

"I'll call you whatever you want if you'd just fuck me already."

I was on a hair trigger here, and my voice was shaking with the effort of holding myself back. Gripping my cock, she jacked me a few times before lining the tip up with her opening. Eyes fixed on mine, she slowly lowered herself down until our hips met.

Her tight heat squeezed me as she began to move up and down, starting slowly but quickly picking up speed. I gripped her hips in my hands and bent my knees for leverage, pushing up to meet her with every downward stroke. One of Steph's hands moved to tweak her clit.

"That's right," I encouraged. "Get there."

Steph's eyes squeezed shut and her face screwed up with pleasure as we both grew closer to completion. Her hair, no longer contained in a ponytail, fanned out over her shoulders in long waves.

"You're fucking beautiful like this, riding my cock like a goddess."

I felt the tremors around my cock as she reached her orgasm, and the minute it started, I let myself go. I groaned her name as I pushed up, releasing my seed into the condom, imagining myself painting the walls of her womb instead of the inside of a piece of latex. Steph shuddered on top of me, biting her lip in pleasure.

She collapsed on my chest with a sigh as I drove into her a few more times, coming longer than I thought was even possible at my age.

Wrapping my arms around her, I held her close while we both fought to get our breath under control. When she slipped off me, I sat up and tied off the condom, wrapping it in a Kleenex, then pulling Steph close.

She shivered as our sweat cooled, prompting me to sit up again and grab the comforter.

"Will you stay over?"

With any other woman I would just assume she'd sleep over, but Steph was not any other woman.

"I should go back to my place," she said sleepily.

I'd never seen her look so relaxed. It made her look younger. More carefree. I felt unaccountably pleased as she burrowed into my side and fell asleep in my arms.

A few hours later I woke with a start. Steph was sliding herself downward in an attempt to move out from beneath my grasp.

"Where are you going?" I grumbled, my voice thick with sleep.

She froze. "Um. I have to go to the bathroom."

"It's across the hall. Are you coming back?"

"I'm not one for sleepovers," she prevaricated. I could sense her reluctance to leave, despite her words.

"I'll make you a deal."

"What?"

"You come on back here when you're done, and I'll reward you."

She stood up, beautifully naked, and gave me a suspicious look. "Reward me how?"

"I'm going to kiss every inch of your delectable body, and when you're so revved up that you're ready to beg, I'll let you choose how I make you come."

"Really?" Her voice sounded choked.

"Lady's choice," I promised.

I held my breath during the ensuing pause.

"I'll be back in three minutes," she finally said. "Be ready."

Steph

I woke up sweating. At first I thought I'd developed a fever or something, but then I realized I was basically surrounded by a wall of man. Christopher was spooning me from behind, his chin resting on my shoulder, my ass nestled into his groin, the front of his legs against the back of mine. I was using one arm as a pillow and he had the other one wrapped over my waist, his fingers splayed across the soft swell of my abdomen.

I couldn't decide whether I felt trapped or protected, and that indecision was alarming.

"Stop thinking," Christopher grumbled from behind me. "It's too early for thinking."

Damn, how did he know I was even awake? I hadn't moved a muscle.

"What time is it?" I asked. His blackout curtains were closed, preventing me from guestimating the time.

He reached behind us and grabbed his phone.

"Six a.m."

"Oh crap! I need to go."

"We don't have to be at the tabletop exercise until nine," he reminded me.

"I need to get my workout done."

"You don't need to work out," he said, squeezing the nearest breast. "You're perfect just the way you are."

"I work out every day," I told him. He groaned as I slid away from him.

"What do you do?" he asked curiously. "To work out, I mean?"

"I run three miles every morning and then do weight exercises and finish up with some yoga."

"You do?"

"Yeah."

He looked adorably rumpled. His thick hair was sticking out in multiple directions, his eyes were squinting, and his jaw was shadowed with whiskers. He sat up.

"Do you want me to join you?" he asked with very little enthusiasm.

I leaned forward and patted his cheek. "Go back to sleep. I prefer to work out alone. I'll see you at nine."

He was snoring softly before I'd finished dressing.

After going back to my place to change into workout gear, I hit the road for my run. I'd woken up feeling tense, mostly because it had felt unexpectedly nice to wake up in Christopher's arms, and that was something I definitely could not let myself get used to. As my feet pounded out a steady rhythm on the pavement, my anxious mind settled.

I'd started running in high school, joining the track team as a way to stay out of the house as much as possible. I wasn't the best runner on the team, but I was definitely the most stubborn, and I'd developed a lifelong running habit that not only helped me stay fit and trim, but also helped me keep my focus and manage stress.

Returning to my temporary apartment, I moved through my weight sequence, then relaxed into several long stretches. By the time I showered and got down to the community center for our training exercise, I felt much more like myself. Until I saw Katy.

"You had sex!" she said the minute she saw me.

My mouth dropped open, and I looked around to make sure we were alone.

"How did you know?"

"Because you had a little smile on your face. You don't smile."

"I smile."

"Rarely."

I gave my best friend a once-over. "Are you sure that's not a guilty conscience talking?"

One eyebrow arched. "I'll have you know that Andrew was a perfect gentleman. Despite my efforts to convince him otherwise."

We both burst out laughing.

"Those Lawson men are quite appealing," I noted as we worked together to arrange the tables for the exercise. "They grow them all kinds of sexy up here."

"No kidding," Katy responded with a laugh. "I almost wish I was staying in town longer so I could wear Andrew down."

"I can't believe you offered him a night of no-strings sex and he said no. What guy does that?"

No strings was all Katy ever offered. Like me, she eschewed relationships.

"Honestly, I don't know which one of us was more shocked," she confided. "He told me he liked me too much to sleep with me. What does that even mean?"

"No clue."

My thoughts returned to the Lawson Lightning Bolt conversation yesterday, and I rolled my eyes at myself. Katy and Andrew weren't going to realize they were soulmates any more than me and Christopher. Even if I'd had the best sex of my life last night. Twice.

Our gab fest was interrupted by Marianne. There was no way we were discussing anything about Andrew or Christopher in front of their mother. She'd probably be fine with it, but she'd also get ideas. Ideas about us staying here and settling down with her "boys". I liked Christopher's mother, and I didn't want to disappoint her.

Marianne jumped right in to help set things up, asking questions about the plan for the day. She was eager to make sure that Lawson was prepared for anything that might happen, and I appreciated her commitment to the project. I only wished everyone I came into contact with would take disaster planning as seriously as she did.

Christopher rolled into the room at ten before nine, his brother Patrick and the high school principal right behind him. Christopher's hair was damp, and he'd shaved since I'd seen him this morning. He strode right up to me, stepping a little too close into my space for a work acquaintance.

"How was your workout?" he asked softly, his eyes boring into mine in a way that made me shiver.

"Great. I feel like a new woman."

"I like the old one just fine," he whispered before moving away to take his seat.

As Katy and I began the training, my eyes kept finding his. I had a feeling that sleeping with him was a big mistake. I didn't want to lead him on, and I'd known going in that his feelings were stronger than mine.

Are they? an annoying little voice in my head asked.

Damned if I knew.

Christopher

By the time we finished our day, it was snowing like crazy. After a quick debate, Katy decided to stay over another day, much to my mother's delight.

"Hopefully Andrew can charm her tonight," she whispered to me. "Then I'll have two of you taken care of."

"You don't need to take care of anything," I said firmly, neglecting to share that my brother had texted me this morning that he liked Katy but had decided that their geographic differences were going to be too much of a barrier. If Katy was too broken up about it, she wasn't letting on as far as I could tell.

I headed over to my office at the Municipal Building to work on a few things before dinner. Steph's training had been good – better than I'd expected honestly – but it had taken the entire day. We'd even had a working lunch. I needed to at least check out my email or I'd never sleep tonight.

After taking care of a few things that couldn't wait, I stopped by the diner and picked up two of the Tuesday specials: meatloaf with mashed potatoes and gravy, buttered green beans, and a biscuit. I hadn't got to spend any time alone with Steph today, but I was hoping I could entice her to hang out with me.

She opened the door of the apartment as soon as I knocked. She was wearing flannel pajama pants with daisies on them, a baggy sweatshirt, and thick wool socks. Her long brown hair hung loose around her shoulders. She looked cute as hell.

"Dinner?" I asked, holding up the bag in my hand.

"What is it?" she sniffed.

"Maddie's Famous Meatloaf, the Tuesday special at the diner."

When she didn't respond right away I added, "I guarantee you it's the best meatloaf in town."

She laughed. "And is there a lot of meatloaf in town?"

"You'd be surprised. Can I come in? Our dinner's getting cold."

"How about I come over there?" she countered.

I suspected she wanted to be sure she could leave whenever she wanted. I knew that she'd wanted to bolt last night right after the first time we made love. I took great pride in the fact that after the second time, she was too exhausted to move.

"Sure. My place is bigger anyway."

She pulled on some boots, tucking her pajama pants into the boots, then grabbed her coat, phone, and keys, following me to my place. Despite the overwhelming desire I had to boost her on the counter and spear her with my already half hard cock, I focused on setting the table for dinner.

After we'd plated the food, I sent her a smile.

"That training wasn't as bad as I expected."

She burst out laughing. "That's high praise there, mister."

"Look Steph, I owe you an apology. I still don't like the idea of those damned bureaucrats in Denver coming up here and telling us what to do..."

"I'm a bureaucrat from Denver," she reminded me.

"True. And you've convinced me that I was wrong. My resistance to creating a plan was...short-sighted. My ego could have led to catastrophe if something major happened."

She fell back in her chair, melodramatically clutching her heart. "Oh my God, did Christopher Lawson just admit that he was wrong about something? Thank God I was sitting down for this."

I nodded. "I'm man enough to admit when I'm wrong."

Her eyes turned dark as she ran her gaze over my chest. I felt her gaze like a caress.

"You're man enough, all right. Maybe you'd like to show me your manliness after dinner."

"Maybe I would."

She wasn't pushing me away. With Steph, that felt like progress.

We spent the rest of dinner chatting, until I realized something crucial: every time I asked a question about anything personal, Steph managed to subtly turn it back to me.

"Tell me about your brother."

"He's great. What was it like growing up with two brothers of your own?"

"They were—." I raised my palm. "Wait, how do you do that?"

"Do what?" she asked.

"Turn all of my questions back on me."

Her look was as neutral as always. In fact, that neutral mask rarely slipped for more than a second, other than when she was in the throes of an orgasm.

"I don't know what you mean."

"Yes, you do."

I pinned her with my gaze, keeping my expression stern, but she just stared back at me. I wondered, not for the first time, what she was thinking.

"Tell me something real," I said huskily. "One thing."

"What do you mean?"

"We've spent a lot of time together the last couple of weeks, Steph. I've been so deep inside you I couldn't tell where you started, and I ended. And yet you still feel like a stranger. Can you give me something? Please?"

I suspected the 'please' was what got her because there was a flicker in her expression. She leaned her elbow on the table, then rested her chin in her hand, giving me a considering look.

"My brother Nathan is two years younger than me," she finally said. "We were always really close growing up, and he followed me to Denver. Graduated a year early, in fact, so he could get there faster."

I sensed there was a story to that, but I didn't pry, asking instead, "Are you still close?"

"Yeah." Her lips quirked in one corner. "Super close. I'm probably a little too motherly with him even though he's a grown man. He always tended to be a little anxious, and I acted as a parent to him in many ways."

"Is he married?"

"No, but he's got a long-distance thing going with this great woman named Liz," she replied. "It's pretty recent, but I don't know how long that's going to last. Between the distance and their work schedules, he's frustrated that they never get to see each other. I think it's especially hard right now because they're in that 'new love' phase where they want to see each other all the time. She's actually perfect for him, so I'm hoping they find a way to make it work."

"Long distance relationships are hard," I acknowledged. "But not impossible."

A long look passed between us before she spoke again.

"I'm not one for relationships, long distance or not."

I recognized the warning in her words and ignored it.

"I have a proposal for you."

"What?" She looked wary.

"I...like you and I think you like me. Clearly we are a good match physically," I said. "Let's agree to be together while you're here. You can teach me more about disaster planning and I'll make you come your brains out at least twice every night."

"Wow, twice a night? That's some confidence you have there."

"It's justified. As I think you saw last night."

"We'll be together just while I'm here?" she clarified. "No other expectations?"

"If that's all you can give me right now Steph, I'm willing to take it."

I didn't add that I was going to do everything in my power to change her mind and figure out a way we could be together for the rest of our lives.

She cocked her head, her expression turning coy.

"In that case, how about we get started on the coming my brains out part?"

Steph

"Tomorrow is Valentine's Day."

I lifted my head from resting on my new favorite place – Christopher's bare chest. We'd been together the last eight nights, including the first night we'd slept together. I'd even stayed in Lawson last weekend instead of going back to Denver. There had been a blizzard, and while I would have made it back okay, it was a good excuse to spend the weekend with Christopher. Mostly in bed.

"Yeah, I know. Poor Nathan. He planned this whole Valentine's Day thing for him and Liz and Denver, but she can't get out of the mountains to join him."

"Do you want to go out to dinner or something?" Christopher asked. "For Valentine's I mean?"

I studied him for a few seconds. "The truth?"

"Always."

"I'm not a romantic person. At all."

"That's shocking," he said drily.

"I hate stuff like Valentine's Day. If you...like someone, then you shouldn't need some fancy romantic crap to prove it."

His chest was rumbling when I set my head back down.

"I hate Valentine's Day too," he confessed. "I know that's true for many guys though."

"It's definitely a girlie holiday," I agreed. "Although my baby brother has a sentimental side that's coming out now that he's in love."

"Can I ask you something?" His voice was soft, like he thought he'd spook me.

"Yeah."

"You told my mother once that your mom was dead. What about your father? Was he in the picture?"

I felt myself tense up, and so did he, because he gave me a squeeze. I willed myself to relax, pushing the bad memories towards the back of my mind where they couldn't bother me.

"He and our mother were married and living together when Nathan and I grew up, if that's what you're asking."

I could practically feel him formulating his next question and decided to save him the trouble.

"My father's been in prison since I was in college. We don't have a relationship. I'd prefer not to talk about it anymore than that."

I couldn't bring myself to explain that he was in prison because he'd killed my mother in a drunken rage.

Christopher was silent for a moment before he said, "Okay. Did I ever tell you about my father?"

I let out a breath of relief at the change of topic. "No."

"He was a big guy. Big physically, big personality. He was the mayor before me, in fact."

"He was?"

"Yeah. He fell in love with my mother the second he laid eyes on her and was still in love with her the day he died." Christopher's voice turned rough. "He died of a heart attack about ten years ago. It was...unexpected."

I wrapped my arm around his torso and gave him a squeeze. "I'm sorry."

"He and I had very similar personalities."

"Grumpy and arrogant?" I teased softly.

"He was the original Mayor Mc Grumpy," he confirmed. "But beneath his gruff exterior, he had a heart of gold."

I pressed a kiss on his pec, right over his heart. "Definitely similar."

"After he died, everyone kind of assumed I'd move into the mayor role."

"Why you and not one of your brothers?" I asked curiously. "Andrew is a lawyer, wouldn't he be the obvious choice?"

"Ever since the town was founded, the eldest Lawson son has served as mayor."

"That's a lot of pressure."

And sexist, I thought to myself. Then again, I hadn't met any female Lawsons, so maybe there were only sons in their family.

"Yeah. But I love this community and I'm glad to give back. Most days."

"What happens if there's no Lawson son to take your place?"

He shrugged. "Honestly, I was never too interested in having kids. So it'll be up to my brothers to produce the next mayor, although as my mother keeps telling us, we're all running out of time."

"Or someone else in town could step up and be mayor."

"That would be nice."

His voice was almost wistful, confirming my suspicion that he really didn't like his job that much.

"Then you could live your life for yourself."

He was quiet for so long I thought he'd fallen asleep, until he cleared his throat.

"I know we agreed to take this day by day," Christopher said. "But I want to be honest with you. I want more."

I sat up to face him, sitting cross legged on the bed. I was wearing one of Christopher's tee shirts and nothing else. I didn't want to examine how much I loved wearing his clothes.

"I'm not a 'more' kind of woman, Christopher. And even if I was, I live in Denver."

"You said you work at home a lot."

"Yeah, we moved to hybrid during the pandemic and given the dearth of office space at the Capitol, I mostly telework if I'm not out in the field or attending meetings in the community. But I also have to be easily accessible for emergencies," I explained. "If I were to live someplace farther away – like Lawson for example – it would be too hard to get to the Emergency Command Center in Denver quickly, especially in the winter."

Christopher looked sad.

"My life is in Denver and your entire life is here in Lawson. There's no sense in either one of us thinking this can be more than it is, no matter how either of us might feel. I'm sorry."

I replayed the conversation in my head several times the next morning on my run.

I'd never felt this way about a guy before. The more time I spent with Christopher, the more I was feeling, well, feelings. And that was a problem. Growing up in an abusive home with a mother who was steadfast in her love for her abuser, I'd developed a skewed sense of love. Love was something that kept you from taking care of yourself. Something that led to bad decisions. If I'd ever doubted that, being with Christopher had confirmed it for me. Because there was a not-so-small part of me that wanted nothing more than to figure out a way that we could be together long-term, regardless of the consequences.

I'd worked way too hard to create my own life and get ahead in a male-dominated career to just throw it all away on a guy, no matter how I felt about him. And I knew there was no way Christopher was going to give up his life in Lawson for me. That would be just as stupid. He was part of the fabric of this community.

Coincidentally it was the same dilemma my brother was facing. He was in love with a woman who had a house and a business in Pine Bluff, but he had a house and a job in Denver. Funny how our lives were mirroring each other.

The Holly siblings were clearly cursed in the relationship department. I had another week of work left in Lawson. As I ran back towards my temporary home, I resolved to just enjoy the time we had left together. There was no sense in pining over Christopher and what could never be.

Christopher

It was Steph's last couple of days in Lawson, and we were no closer to figuring out how to be together than we'd been when we had that talk the night before Valentine's Day.

I was hopelessly in love with her, and while she hadn't said the words, I was certain she was in love with me too. She hadn't opened up to me about her past, but it was clear there was a lot of trauma there. Then again, it wasn't her past keeping us apart, it was her present. And mine too.

Over the past few weeks, I'd come to respect Steph and the work she did. She was one of the people who ran towards a disaster instead of running away. And while it seemed tedious, I'd learned how vitally important this emergency planning work really was. The time to figure out who was doing what really was not during an actual emergency situation. If something major happened in Lawson – God forbid – we would be ready now. And that was one hundred percent thanks to Steph.

"I don't know what to do," I confessed to my brothers over lunch. "She's a bigwig at the State, and she needs to live close to the Capitol. I can't ask her to give that up for me, and even if I did ask, there's no way she would."

"Why does she have to be the one to give everything up?" Patrick asked.

"I'm the mayor here," I reminded him.

"So? It's not like you couldn't get some other job in Denver. Hell, you're fifty years old. You could retire."

"I'm not quite ready to retire," I told him drily. "I have a few good years of work left in me."

"Be a consultant. Get a job that you didn't inherit from your father. Hell, you could go back to being an architect. You really liked that job."

After I'd gotten out of the military, I'd gotten a degree in architecture, and had worked in the field for several years before I took over as mayor.

"There's always McDonald's," Andrew added. "You could flip burgers. They have plenty of fast food places in the big city."

I tossed a french fry across the table, hitting him right between the eyes. But the truth was, I was embarrassed that it hadn't occurred to me that I could be the one to move. Patrick was right. I could get a job in Denver, then Steph could keep her career and we could still be together. It would be a big step though, especially after spending my whole life in this town.

"The question is, do you love her enough to make a big change?" Andrew asked.

"The bigger question is, does she love me enough for me to make a change."

"Well, you'll never know if you don't talk about it."

Despite that sage advice, I was a total chickenshit and avoided the topic until Thursday, Steph's last night in town. She had finished all her planning work and had helped me submit the appropriate paperwork to both the county and state. The only thing left to do was for us to present the plan to the Town Council at their meeting the following morning, then Steph would be headed back to Denver for good.

"Do you need to come back here periodically and check on our planning?" my mother asked late Thursday afternoon. The question was directed at Steph, but her gaze was fixed on mine.

Mom had been steadily dropping hints that I needed to do something about the Steph situation. She was as terrified that I'd let her get away as I was.

"No," Steph answered. "Once the local jurisdictions are trained, we expect them to keep up with updating plans and doing annual preparedness training on their own."

I studied her face. As usual, Steph's expression was blank, but now I knew her well enough to read her eyes. She looked troubled.

"So you're just heading back to Denver then?" Mom asked, giving us both a disapproving look. "That's it?"

"It's where I live, Marianne," Steph reminded her. "My job is in Denver, this was always going to be temporary."

"At least stay until Saturday," Mom bargained. "We can have one last dinner together before you disappear." Mom sent me a meaningful look before adding, "Forever."

"Thanks Marianne. I've been so grateful for your work on this project, and most importantly your hospitality towards me, but I really need to get back to the city. I'll be driving home after the town council meeting tomorrow morning."

Steph looked everywhere but at me. Mom sighed deeply, then threw up her hands and stalked out of the room without another word.

"What's wrong with your mom?" Steph asked. "She seems annoyed."

"She's mad that I'm not begging you to stay here."

"Why would you do that?" she asked lightly.

"You know why."

Steph sighed, not even pretending to not understand.

"Christopher, we knew what this was going in."

"I know." I stepped closer, placing my hands on her shoulders until she looked up at me. "My feelings for you haven't changed, Steph. If anything, now that I've gotten to know you better, I'm even more in love with you than I was when we first got together. The question is, are things different for you?"

She nodded, then shook her head, then nodded again, her expression turning conflicted.

"I...well, I care for you Christopher. I care for you a lot. But it doesn't matter, because this thing with us can never work out."

"Because we live too far away from each other?"

She nodded. "Sure. That. Our lives are in very different places. I'm not giving up a career I fought so hard for."

I knew instinctively that our living arrangements and her job weren't the only issue.

"What if I moved to Denver?"

"You're the mayor, and you've lived here your entire life. You can't just uproot your life. We've known each other a month. This isn't some Hallmark Christmas movie. It's real life."

"I have no idea what a Hallmark Christmas movie has to do with this. I thought Hallmark was that store in the mall where you buy birthday cards?"

"You've never seen a Hallmark Christmas movie?" For a second, she looked flummoxed.

"No."

"They're these sweet cheesy holiday romance movies that all have the exact same plot. Someone from the city comes to a small town and falls in love over the holidays. Then the city person moves to the small town, and they live happily ever after. Oh, and there's usually a matchmaking mother or grandma and a wisecracking best friend helping them get together. Sometimes a dog. Or an old man who really turns out to be Santa."

"Those sound like terrible movies."

One corner of her mouth quirked up. "They're terribly awesome."

This was unexpected. I had no idea that Steph liked romantic movies. It felt like I'd just unlocked a new clue about her.

"In this case the small-town person is offering to come to the city."

"I'm not cut out for forever," she whispered, her voice small. "You need to find someone who's better for you. I'm too...damaged for love."

"Bullshit."

She jumped at my forceful tone.

"You're not damaged. You're scared."

"What if I am?" she retorted. "It doesn't change anything."

"So that's it then? You're not willing to even try to figure something out? We just have tonight?"

"Yeah."

For a minute I thought she was going to cry, but then she blinked quickly, clearing the sheen in her eyes.

"I'm sorry Christopher, truly I am. But we just have tonight."

Steph

"You two are even gloomier than usual."

I looked up at my friend Carmen. She owned a fabulous Italian restaurant where Nathan and I usually met for dinner a few times a month. Carmen and I used to live in the same apartment building and had become fast friends when we were both training for a marathon with the local running club.

"Hey Car, how are you?"

Carmen plopped into the booth, shoving me over with her hip. She glanced between me and my brother, who was sitting on the other side of the booth with a sad look on his face.

"I'm fine. What are you two pouting about?"

"Nathan's in love."

Carmen's face lit up. "That's great!"

When neither of us responded, her expression sobered.

"So what's the problem? She doesn't like good looking slightly neurotic bureaucrats?"

"She lives up in Pine Bluff," Nathan said dejectedly. "And between the snow and our opposite schedules, we haven't seen each other in *weeks.*"

"Wait. You have a girl you love, who loves you back...," she waited for Nathan's nod. "And the only problem is that you live too far apart?"

"Yeah."

"Well fix it," she said pragmatically.

"It's not that easy," Nathan said. "Our entire lives are in two different places."

"It's exactly that easy. Can you move closer? Can you both live in the middle somewhere? Can you telework? Get a new job? Can she?"

Nathan looked thoughtful. "You know what? I actually might be able to telework." He jumped out of his seat. "Sis, I need to..."

"Go." I waved him off. "Dinner's on me. Figure out how to go make it work with Liz."

As Nathan hurried away, Carmen moved to the seat he'd vacated, pinning me with a hard stare.

"What's your problem? Are you in love too?"

"Um..."

Carmen reared back in surprise.

"Holy shit, I was just kidding. I didn't know you'd met someone. Tell Aunt Carmen everything."

"I went to this little town called Lawson because the mayor kept refusing to do their state-mandated emergency plan, and the Governor wanted it done," I explained. "The minute I saw him I felt...well, something. He's big and stubborn and growly but also kind of sweet, you know? At first, we were fighting, butting heads all the time, and then somehow we were kissing."

"That's hot."

"It was. Until he ruined it by saying he was falling in love with me."

'That asshole," Carmen joked.

"I told him I could only give him one night, but then one night turned to three weeks and somehow I was spending all my time in Lawson."

"I was wondering why I hadn't seen you for a while," Carmen said. "I thought you were doing something disaster related that I hadn't heard about."

"Oh, it was a disaster all right," I said miserably. "Because by the time I was done with the project, I wanted nothing more than to throw away everything I'd ever worked for, quit my job, and spend the rest of my time in podunk Lawson. But I'm not going to do that."

"How did you leave it with him?" Carmen asked.

"We talked and agreed it wouldn't work." I hesitated. "Well I agreed, he seemed to think there was some solution we could figure out."

"I can't believe that you and your brother both traveled for work and fell in love with someone in a small town within months of each other. What are the chances?"

"I didn't say I fell in love."

She stared at me silently, one dark eyebrow raised in a way that I knew was a carbon copy of her Italian mother.

"Okay fine. I'm in love with him. But that doesn't change anything."

"What happened after you had the 'this will never work' conversation?" she asked.

"We spent one last night together fucking like it was our last night on Earth, then I slipped out early in the morning while he was still sleeping and drove back to Denver. I thought it was best to make a clean break."

"That was kind of shitty, Stephanie Marie," she chided.

I winced. "I know. I chickened out. I didn't want to deal with a long drawn-out goodbye."

"Have you heard from him since?"

"Yeah, he texted me a couple of times, saying he missed me and stuff like that."

"What did you say?"

"I missed him too, but there was no sense in us dragging things out. I told him we needed to make a clean break, and I haven't responded since then."

Carmen leaned back in her seat with a huff. "Do you have any idea how much I'd love to have a handsome, caring man who loves me? Someone with a job and all his own teeth?"

"No."

"It's one of my top three life goals," she said wistfully. "I'm going to give you the same advice I gave your brother: fix this. It's really not that complicated."

I shook my head sadly. "I can't. I'm not a relationship person. It'll never work out between us."

"Bullshit."

"It's true."

"Then I guess you're doomed to live alone with a bunch of cats."

"I don't really like cats."

Carmen pushed to standing. "You're hopeless."

Christopher

Three weeks later...

"It's official. You're no longer the mayor."

"I can't believe you mounted a recall campaign against me, Mom," I said, looking at the document she handed me. It was signed by the Chief Elections Officer, also known as my Aunt Mary, declaring that I was officially relieved of my mayoral duties.

"It's for your own good. Now you get your ass down to Denver and figure things out with your girlfriend before I repossess your house."

"I don't think you can do that Mom. Only the bank can."

"I'm the Acting Mayor now, I'll run this town as I see fit."

It was ironic. In some ways Mom had been running this town for years, even back when my father was mayor. She just hadn't had the title.

"All that effort was for nothing, Mom. I've already got this handled." I reached over to the counter behind me, grabbing a sheaf of paperwork that had been delivered today. "I'd already accepted a job at an architecture firm."

My mother scanned the documents, a delighted look on her face. "This pays more than being mayor."

"Yep."

"And it's in Denver."

"Yep."

"Does Steph know?"

I shook my head. "She's not responding to my texts anymore. I guess I'm going to need to head down to Denver and hang out at the Capitol until I find her and convince her to give us a chance."

"You don't need to do that," Mom said. "I have her home address."

"You do?"

"Yep," she said, imitating me with a cheeky grin. "I told her I needed it to send her a Christmas card."

"Christmas is nine months away."

"Let's just say I had faith that you'd get your head out of your ass and figure out a way to get your girl."

"I'm heading out in the morning, Mom." I reached down and pulled her into a tight hug. "Thanks for your help."

"Good luck."

The next morning, I drove down the mountain towards Denver, my trunk stuffed with boxes. Even if Steph rejected me, I still needed to spend some time in the city figuring out my living arrangements before I started my new job. I just hoped we were going to do that together.

"The destination is on your right."

I slowed down as the robotic voice of the GPS indicated that I'd arrived at the address my mother had given me. I parked on the curb, taking a second to study the house. It was a cute Craftsman style place, set back from the street a bit with a neatly manicured lawn. Two rocking chairs sat on the porch, a small table between them.

Taking a deep breath, I strode up the walkway to knock on the door, then stepped back in surprise when a man opened the door before I got there. He was good-looking, about ten years younger than me, with dark hair and dark eyes. He looked vaguely familiar.

"Who are you?" I asked, my voice harsh. Surely Steph hadn't found someone new already?

He frowned. "Who are *you*?"

"I'm Christopher Lawson."

The man's face broke out in a smile.

"Took you long enough."

He reached out to shake my hand.

"I'm Nathan Holly, Steph's brother. I'd love to get acquainted, but I've got my own girl to get."

He stepped past me, then stopped, looking almost nervously at the open front door before lowering his voice.

"She'd kill me for telling you this, but our childhood was...difficult. Our father...hurt our mother. Hurt us too, although Steph always took the brunt of it."

I felt a flare of white hot anger.

"Steph's always been the one who's been there for me, my whole life. She's my best friend and my protector."

Nathan's voice hardened as he met my eyes. He puffed up his chest assertively.

"If you ever hurt her, you will regret it. I won't stop coming for you until I ruin your life. I won't kill you, I'll just make you wish you were dead."

I resisted the urge to shiver. This guy was a little intense.

"Understood. But I won't hurt her. I give you my word."

Nathan nodded thoughtfully, his expression softening. "Good. Tell my sister I'll call her from Pine Bluff."

I watched him head towards a car in the driveway and pull out, looking cheerful.

"Nate? Was someone at the door?"

I looked up as Steph appeared in the doorway, looking adorable in faded jeans that hugged her curves, and a snug black tee shirt from the Denver Marathon. Her dark hair was piled on top of her head in a messy knot.

"Christopher?" She looked at me in shock. "What are you doing here?"

Steph

To say that seeing Christopher Lawson standing on my porch was a surprise would be the understatement of the century. I hadn't heard from him in two weeks, probably because I'd been ignoring his texts. I figured he'd given up on me and yet, here he was.

He was wearing faded jeans and a navy blue City of Lawson logo tee shirt that hugged his broad frame. I loved that shirt. The last time I'd seen it I'd been wearing it while he leaned me over a counter and took me from behind.

"Can I come in?" he asked.

I nodded, moving back to allow him entrance. He stepped into the living room, looking around curiously.

"Do you, um, do you want something to drink?"

"I wouldn't mind a water."

He followed me to the kitchen, and I poured us each a glass of water from the pitcher I kept in the refrigerator, setting one on each side of the kitchen table. Christopher looked nervous, something I'd never seen before. We sat across the table from each other, completely silent, until I repeated my earlier question.

"What are you doing here, Christopher?"

I didn't need to ask how he'd gotten my address. I knew that Marianne must have given it to him.

"I miss you. I hate every minute of being away from you."

My heart squeezed. "There's no sense in making this harder than it needs to be. Some things are just not meant to be."

"What if they are? Meant to be, I mean."

When I didn't answer he added, "I got a job. Here in Denver."

"What?"

"I'm moving to Denver." He spoke slowly and softly, like he was trying not to spook a skittish horse. "I want to be with you. So much so that I'm willing to uproot my entire life to make it happen."

My mouth dropped open in shock.

"I'm not saying I need to move in here with you," he rushed to add. "But it took me fifty years to find the love of my life. I don't want to spend any more time away from her. I need you, Steph, and I think you need me too."

I felt a jolt of happiness, quickly followed by a sense of panic. I leapt out of my chair and paced towards the refrigerator. When I turned around, he was right behind me. For such a big guy, Christopher was really light on his feet.

He placed one big hand on each of my shoulders. "Breathe."

I exhaled sharply, and he moved one hand to cup my left cheek. I couldn't help but lean into his warmth. I loved it when he touched me like that.

"I love you, Steph. It's okay if you're not there yet, but at least give us a chance. A chance at forever."

I shook my head, my throat tightening. "I can't."

He stared at me so long I started to squirm.

"I won't hurt you, Steph. Physically or emotionally. I'm not your father or any other guy. You know me. You know what's in my heart. I've never held anything back with you."

"Damn that Nathan," I grumbled.

My brother had been pushing me to reach out to Christopher. Ever since he'd decided he was going to move up to Pine Bluff with Liz he'd been encouraging me to face my feelings for Christopher. He'd even come over this morning to nag me about it again.

"Someday you'll tell me more, when you're ready," Christopher continued as if I hadn't spoken. "All I'm asking from you right now is that you give us a chance. Look into your heart, be honest about your feelings, and give us a chance. Can you do that?"

Without any conscious thought, I felt my head bob up and down. Christopher looked so relieved it nearly broke my heart. Maybe this was a mistake, but damned if it didn't feel right.

"What about your job in Lawson? You're the mayor."

"Not anymore."

"You quit?" I asked in shock.

He shook his head. "I was planning to quit, but then my mother led a recall campaign and got me booted out of office."

I rolled in my lips to keep from laughing. "Why would she do that?"

"She told me that she figured it was the only way I would get my head out of my ass and come get my girl." His eyes sparkled with amusement. "But the joke was on her, because I'd already lined up a job at an architectural firm here in Denver."

"Really?"

"Yeah, really. I still had a lot of connections in the architecture field and my old firm was glad to take me back. They have an office here."

"So you're moving to Denver?" I confirmed, even though he'd told me like three times already. It felt too good to be true.

"Yeah."

"What about your house in Lawson?"

"I'll keep it. The mortgage payment is pretty low. I could rent it out, but I figured we could make it our weekend retreat."

"You've given this a lot of thought," I noted.

He backed me up a few steps until my hips hit the counter next to the refrigerator. Wrapping his hands around my waist, Christopher boosted me up and slid between my legs, carefully watching my reaction. My body responded to his nearness immediately, my nipples tightening and a rush of arousal flooding my panties.

"Are you sure you'll be happy in Denver?" I asked. "What if this is all a terrible mistake?"

"I'd be happy living in the seventh circle of hell if I was with you."

I burst out laughing. "Wow, that's quite a commitment."

He leaned closer, giving me a soft, quick kiss on the lips. "Someday I'll make a more permanent commitment. When you're ready."

"Hell's pretty permanent."

"So is marriage."

When I opened my mouth to respond he claimed my lips in a kiss that was rough and deep and everything I needed to settle my soul. When he finally pulled back, we were both breathing heavily.

"Say it again," I asked softly.

"Which part?" he asked.

"The part about how you love me."

His eyes darkened. "I love you, Steph. More than I can say."

I took a deep breath and for the first time in my life I said the words I'd only ever said to my little brother. "I love you too."

Christopher looked like he'd won the damned lottery.

"I'm so glad I refused to do my emergency plan."

I laughed. "You wouldn't have been saying that if you'd had an earthquake or something before I got there."

"How about we go create our own earthquake?" he suggested, pressing his hard cock against my core. I rolled my hips in response.

"Why Mr. Lawson, are you trying to get into my pants?"

"You won't be wearing pants for long, baby," he promised, boosting me up to his waist and wrapping my legs around him.

"You know I hate diminutives," I reminded him with no heat.

"Yeah, but you love me." He sounded smug, but I'd give him this.

"You're right. I do."

Epilogue—Christopher

Seven months later...

"I can't believe my baby brother got married."

I looked up from reading to see Steph standing in the bedroom doorway wearing sleep shorts and a tank top, her pert little nipples pressing against the thin fabric. As always, the sight of her made my dick twitch and my heart rate speed up just a little bit.

We'd come up to Pine Bluff for Nathan and Liz's wedding. It had been a nice celebration in the park, with everyone in town celebrating the newlyweds. I'd spent quite a bit of time with Nathan and Liz since Steph and I had officially become a couple, and they were both awesome.

But not as awesome as my fiancé. That's right, two months ago I'd proposed to Steph on the sixth anniversary of the day we'd met. I might not be the most romantic guy in the world, but I'd go to my grave remembering the day I'd looked up from my budget report and saw the Lawson Lightning Bolt in the form of one Stephanie Holly.

"You do remember your 'baby brother' is forty years old, right?" I teased her.

"Forty-one," she corrected, stalking towards the bed with a gleam in her eye. "How about you take off those pants and give me a ride."

Steph loved nothing more than to be on top of me, and just the thought of it made me instantly hard. I tossed my book and reading glasses onto the side table, then lifted my hips to whip off my sleep pants. My eager cock bounced up towards my stomach as I slid down to my back. Stef climbed on the bed, throwing one leg over my hips, and rubbing her already wet pussy against my shaft.

Leaning forward, she caught my lips with hers, kissing me long and hard.

I could hardly believe that things were still so hot between us. We'd had sex more days than not over the last seven months, both of us seemingly unable to get enough of the other.

After Steph agreed to give us a chance, I'd made an admittedly half-hearted effort to find a place of my own until the night when Steph had suddenly looked up at me across the dinner table and given me a stern look.

"Hey. You're living here. How did that happen?"

"Um. Well, you invited me to stay over that first night I was in town," I reminded her. "Then you kept inviting me to stay."

"You're a sneaky bastard," she said with no heat.

"I can't believe you're just realizing that I've been here every night for the past six weeks," I'd teased.

"You've got me totally brainless from the orgasms," she'd responded. "Well, as long as your shit is here, we might as well talk about officially living together."

Our transition hadn't been without bumps – especially since we were both stubborn as hell – but overall, our cohabitation had been better than I ever could have hoped. At least once I'd learned to be a bit neater. I wasn't a slob by any means, but my Type A girlfriend was a bit of a neat freak. Big surprise.

A couple of weekends a month we'd head up to Lawson to see my family and take a break from the hustle and bustle of the city. It worked perfectly for us, and needless to say, my mother was thrilled.

Steph broke the kiss, scooting back to line up my cock with her opening. She kept her eyes glued to mine as she slowly lowered herself until our hips met, my cock sheathed in her wet heat. My favorite place to be.

We both groaned as she began undulating her hips, riding my cock with an abandon that made me even harder than I already was.

"I love you so much," I told her as she ground down on me.

Her smile lit up her face. "I love you too, Mayor Mc Grumpy."

"That's Architect Mc Grumpy now," I reminded her, even though we both knew I'd been significantly less grumpy since we'd gotten together. It was hard to be grumpy when I was living my best life with the woman I loved.

"You're the best disaster I ever worked on," she panted as her movements sped up.

"Right back at you," I gasped.

We both found our release almost simultaneously, then Steph collapsed onto my chest, her head on my shoulder. I wrapped my arms around her, holding her close. Right where I wanted her forever.

***

If you liked this book, please leave a review. Reviews are like puppies, they make everyone feel happy!
Keep on reading for a special preview of Steph's brother Nathan and his girlfriend Liz's story in "Christmas Punch[1]" by Rose Bak.

---

1. https://books2read.com/XmasPunch

Special Preview

Christmas Punch by Rose Bak

"They denied your liquor license? I don't understand. I thought you said it was just a formality?"

I shook my head, even though my best friend Renee couldn't see the movement through the phone.

"I thought it would be. I couldn't believe my eyes when I got the letter. The letter said that they've determined that there's too high of a concentration of liquor-serving establishments here in Pine Bluff."

"I didn't realize there were that many places to booze it up in your tiny little town."

"There's not, that's the weird thing. We have one bar, one tiny little liquor store, and one restaurant that's only allowed to serve beer and wine."

Our dining options were also pretty limited in my small town. It was one of the reasons everyone in town was excited about my idea to open a café and art space. Besides the one restaurant we had a deli that doubled as the post office and a hardware store with a bakery counter in the back – we liked to have multipurpose businesses here in Pine Bluff – that was it. We didn't even have a coffee shop or a pizza place. No one liked having to drive fifteen to twenty minutes to the next town over when they wanted a decent cup of coffee.

For years I'd been itching to find a way to combine my culinary training with my love of music and art. I'd spent most of my adult life raising my kids, helping my ex-husband with his business, and picking up the occasional catering jobs. Now my kids were out on their own, my husband was remarried to a girl half his age, and it was finally "Liz Time". Or it would be if I could convince the faceless bureaucrat at the county to approve my damn liquor license.

He wouldn't be faceless for long though.

"I submitted an official appeal and requested a site visit," I told Renee. "In fact, he's supposed to come today. I posted in the group telling everyone to be on their good behavior."

Pine Bluff had a very active resident-only Facebook page where we shared announcements, news, and local gossip. I'd warned them all not to be too crazy when the liquor license guy got here. Sometimes our little town was a bit over the top and I wanted to make a good impression on the county inspector who apparently thought he'd find a town full of drunks.

"Let me know how it goes," Renee said.

"I will. Now what's new with you?"

"I picked up a new personal chef gig."

Renee and I had met years ago when we were both in our twenties and living in New York City. As the only two women in our culinary training class, we'd bonded immediately. Our friendship had held strong over the years, even after we both got married, had kids, and I moved to Colorado. Hardly a week went by when we didn't check in with each other.

"What's the gig?" I asked.

"I'm going to do cooking lessons for a guy who had a massive heart attack. He needs to learn how to cook something besides microwave burritos and burgers," she explained. "His kids actually hired me. They're worried about him so I'm his Christmas gift. He gets ten cooking lessons at his house, and I'll try to convince him that it's possible to adopt a heart-healthy diet. He's strictly a meat-and-potatoes kind of guy."

"Is he on-board with lessons?"

"Not really. We'd been warned by his kids that he was stubborn, and they weren't kidding. This one's going to be a challenge, I can tell already."

"Well, if anyone can whip him into shape it's you," I laughed.

Renee was the strongest woman I knew. She'd probably been a general in her last life.

I heard the bell ring on the entry door and looked down over the shop from my position up on the mezzanine that separated the first floor retail space from the hallway leading to my upstairs apartment.

"I'll be right down," I called to the man who'd entered.

He looked up and I swear I forgot how to breathe for a minute. He was tall and lean with broad shoulders that strained against his navy blue puffy jacket. His dark hair was short, thick, and neatly styled, framing his strong face. I took in the square jaw that was slightly shadowed with scruff, and the chin dimple that was so deep I could see it from up here. Brown eyes stood out against the slash of his thick eyebrows. He was easily the handsomest guy I'd ever seen in real life.

"Whoa!" I whispered, awestruck.

"What?" Renee asked. "What are you whoa-ing about over there?"

My eyes stayed glued to the stranger's. I'm pretty sure I forgot how to blink.

"I've gotta go, Renee. Someone's here. I'll call you later."

Finally breaking eye contact, I ended the call and made my way to the stairs, realizing belatedly that the hot guy must be the person from the county coming to evaluate my liquor license appeal. He stood in the center of the space, looking around with a disapproving look on his handsome face.

I tried to see the space with fresh eyes. After my divorce, I'd sold my house and bought this retail property on Snowflake Lane, our main street. At one time it had been an industrial site, then someone had separated half of the second level to create an upstairs living quarters. I'd moved into the apartment upstairs and had spent the last six months remodeling the main floor to make it perfect.

It was a large, open space with brick walls and lots of high windows that let in sunlight from above. I'd spent a small fortune to add windows and a retail-style door at the street level, and to build out a small commercial kitchen.

I'd finished the floors myself, spending hours unearthing the natural beauty that had been hidden by concrete tiles and years of dirt. A friend who was a woodworker had designed a lovely display case for baked goods and a countertop area for the cash register and coffee machines. The café tables and chairs had arrived last week and were currently stacked up on one side of the space along with boxes of dishes and cutlery.

In anticipation of a soft opening in mid-December, I'd put up a huge Christmas tree and hung Christmas decorations throughout the space. Even though we weren't open yet, people in town had been stopping by to grab a coffee or sample the baked goods.

To start with, the café would have just a small menu, consisting of mostly artisan sandwiches, special quiches, soups, salads, and baked goods. I was planning to expand the menu later as the business grew. I'd purchased a high-end espresso machine so we could offer specialty coffees and had sourced beans from a Colorado coffee roaster.

The café was going to be open from seven a.m. until two p.m. during the week, with longer hours on weekends. At night we'd offer specialty cocktails along with nighttime musical performances and art shows highlighting local artists. I also planned to rent the space out for events. It was going to be great. But I needed a liquor license for my nighttime offerings.

Liz's Café was beautiful, and I was proud of the space I created. It was a dream come true, me making lemonade out of the lemons of my divorce. I just needed to get this county guy to see my vision.

"You must be Nathan Holly," I said, extending a hand to the man. "I'm Liz Delaney, the owner of Liz's Café."

The man nodded, and when our eyes met again, he looked almost dazed. As he shook my hand, his expression turned into a frown. He released my hand quickly as if I'd burned him. I wondered if he'd felt that odd little jolt when we touched, the same as I did.

He cleared his throat. "Yes, I'm Nathan Holly. This place is very...Christmassy."

It didn't sound like a compliment. By his tone "Christmassy" seemed to be one step above "a rat-infested hovel".

"Christmas is a big holiday here in Pine Bluff," I told him. "We celebrate all month."

The look of distaste crossed his face so quickly I thought I might have imagined it.

"Shall we get down to business?"

***

For more of Nathan's story check out Christmas Punch, available at select online retailers[1].

---

1. *https://books2read.com/XmasPunch*

Other Books by Rose Bak

Boozy Book Club Series
Beach Reads
Bubbly & Billionaires
Martinis & Mysteries
Bourbon & Bikers
Midlife Madness
Extra Innings
Midlife Crisis Romance Series
Summer Wedding
Roasting with Rob
Christmas Punch
Disaster Planning
The Good with Numbers Holiday Romance Series
Love Unmasked
The Thanksgiving Scrooge
Maid for Christmas
Countdown to Love
Valentine's Lottery
Christmas Angel
Loving the Holidays Contemporary Romance Series
Dating Santa
New Year's Steve
Independence Dave
Comfort & Joy
Faking It with the Detective
Dropping the Ball
The Oliver Boys Band Contemporary Romance Series
Until You Came Along
Rock Star Teacher
Rock Star Writer

Rock Star Neighbor
Rock Star Lawyer
Bite-Sized Shifters Paranormal Romance Series
Long Distance Wolf
Wolf Doctor
Kat's Dog
Designer Wolf
Wolf Sheriff
Cocktail Wolf
Second Chance Wolf
Runaway Wolf
Holidays with the Shifters Series
Santa's Claws
Bear Humbug
Jingle Bear
Silver Paws
Joy to the Wolf
Lion's Heart
Magical Midlife Series
Love Potion
Psychic Flashes
Halloween Surprise
Giant Love
The Diamond Bay Contemporary Romance Series
Brand New Penny
Fresh as a Daisy
Right as Rain
Reunited Series
Together Again
Finding My Baby
King of the Reunion
Caught by My Best Friend

Standalones

Saving Texas

Texas Christmas

Factory Reset

Second Chance to Score

The Marriage Solution

Beach Wedding

Jessie's Girl

Non-fiction

What to Do If You Find a Cougar in Your Living Room: Self-Care in an Uncaring World

It's All About Relationships: Reflections on Love, Friendship, and Connection

Catch up with these and other stories coming soon. Join my newsletter for more information[1] or follow my author page on your favorite retailer.

---

1. *https://storyoriginapp.com/giveaways/ba6caac0-d4f9-11ed-80b7-073007e1a152*

About the Author

Rose Bak has been obsessed with books since she got her first library card at age five. She is a passionate reader with an e-reader bursting with thousands of beloved books.

Although Rose enjoys writing both fiction and nonfiction, romance novels have always been her favorite guilty pleasure, both as a reader and an author. Rose's contemporary romance books focus on strong female characters over thirty-five and the alpha males who love them. Expect a lot of steam, a little bit of snark, and a guaranteed happily ever after.

Rose lives in the Pacific Northwest with her family, and special needs dogs. In addition to writing, she also teaches accessible yoga and loves music. Sadly, she has absolutely no musical talent, so she mostly sings in the shower.

Please sign up for the Rose Bak Romance newsletter[1] to get a free book and keep up to date on all the latest news. You can also follow Rose on Facebook[2], Instagram[3], Twitter[4], Goodreads[5], or Bookbub[6].

---

1. https://storyoriginapp.com/giveaways/ba6caac0-d4f9-11ed-80b7-073007e1a152
2. https://www.facebook.com/AuthorRoseBak
3. https://www.instagram.com/authorrosebak/
4. https://twitter.com/AuthorRoseBak
5. https://www.goodreads.com/authorrosebak
6. https://www.bookbub.com/authors/rose-bak

Don't miss out!

Visit the website below and you can sign up to receive emails whenever Rose Bak publishes a new book. There's no charge and no obligation.

https://books2read.com/r/B-A-VATM-AEDHC

BOOKS 2 READ

Connecting independent readers to independent writers.